Gateway to Paradise

Gateway to Paradise

STORIES

MATTHEW VOLLMER

A Karen & Michael Braziller Book

PERSEA BOOKS / NEW YORK

Requests for permission to reprint or to make copies and
for any other information should be addressed to the publisher:

Persea Books, Inc.
277 Broadway
New York, New York 10007

These stories first appeared, often in different form,
in the following venues: "Probation," in *Epoch;*
"Downtime" (as "The Ones You Want to Keep"), in *Unstuck;*
"Dog Lover," in *Willow Springs;* "Scoring," in *The Antioch Review;*
and "Gateway to Paradise," in *The Collagist.*

Library of Congress Cataloging-in-Publication Data
Vollmer, Matthew.
[Short stories. Selections]
Gateway to paradise : stories / Matthew Vollmer.—First edition.
pages ; cm
"A Karen and Michael Braziller Book."
ISBN 978-0-89255-466-9 (alk. paper)
I. Title.
PS3622.O6435A6 2015
813'.6–dc23
2015004902

Design and composition by Rita Lascaro
Typeset in Century Schoolbook
Manufactured in the United States of America

FIRST EDITION

CONTENTS

Gateway to Paradise

Downtime

IN THE ATRIUM of the Park Vista hotel, a glass elevator rose from a fern-shrouded vestibule. Its windows rattled; its lights—softball-sized bulbs bordering its tinted
glass—flickered. Ted Barber, who'd been standing on the
tenth floor watching a boy on the seventh toss paper air-
planes into the lobby, didn't notice the elevator until it
stopped on his level. Then, like a man returning to the
material world after having disappeared inside a prayer,
he raised his head, blinked rapidly, and zeroed in on
the elevator's sole passenger, who, he was surprised to
realize, he recognized. It was his wife, Tavey. She didn't
look good. Then again, she was dead. Her bathing suit
was tattered. Her greenish-blond hair was tangled with
seaweed, her skin peppered with sand and bits of shell-
shards. She limped out of the elevator and rounded the
corner. The wounds on her arms and legs—blistering lash
marks—were oozing.

Ted pointed a finger at her. "No," he said.

Tavey's muck-caked lips parted. Her teeth were white

and smooth and perfectly straight, as if they'd been carved from pearls. "I missed you," she said.

Ted gripped the cracked flesh of the pleather cushion at the top of the retaining wall. "This is not a good time," he said.

"It's not fair. You don't know what it's like."

"I'm not *supposed* to know."

"We're in this together," Tavey replied. She twisted the sopping mass of her hair. Liquid streamed over her body. "We're one flesh. Remember?"

Ted wheeled his suitcase in the opposite direction. No way was he going through this again. Not today. The hotel air—dry and frigid—blazed against his face. His eyes watered. He wanted badly to run, but settled for a brisk stride. He didn't want to give anyone the impression he had anything to flee.

Dr. Theodore Barber—or "Doc," as the citizens of Valleytown, North Carolina, called him—hadn't vacationed in years. He hadn't wanted to. They called it "downtime" for a reason: if you had too much of it, you could fall down a hole in your mind. And so, for the past few years, Ted had preferred to stay as busy as possible, to keep the materials of his trade—amalgams and anesthetics, syringes, gloves, crinkly plastic sacks of autoclaved tools, reclining chairs, and overhead lamps—within reach. Mouths, after all, had saved him. Mouths—where bacteria flourished, where puffy gums bled at the slightest touch, where teeth had been worn down to little eraser-sized nubs, and where incomprehensibly fat tongues slapped against his rubber-gloved fingers—had given him purpose. Any fool could pull a tooth: take a pair of forceps and yank. The problem? It would hurt. A lot. But performing a pain-free extraction? That took a steady hand. Attention to detail. Patience. A second and sometimes third injection of Novocain, if a patient claimed to feel the needle prick when Ted tested gums for sensation. As long as you loosened the tooth by slowly rocking it in its socket, a gentle tug would suffice. Dazed and grateful, the patient, who'd no doubt been raised in these same mountains and suffered at the hands of a less considerate dentist—namely Fred Mintz, who'd owned the practice previously—would shake Ted's hand, and with a mouth stuffed full of bloody gauze, claim to have felt not a thing. Ted felt less proud than relieved. But both relief and satisfaction were short-lived. There were other patients waiting. Other mouths. Other teeth, their decaying roots throbbing. Ted had seen the calendar, turned page after page. For weeks—for *months, years*—there were no open slots to be found.

In room 1002 of the Park Vista, Allison Hart stood upon a king-sized bed. She'd wrapped herself in a sheet. On the room's clock radio, a song warbled: Johnny Cash, singing "Ring of Fire."

"Down, down, down," she crooned. Her hair, a mass of red curls, slapped her cheeks. Gatlinburg had been Allison's idea; she knew it was cheesy, with its ski lifts and shooting galleries, but it was far enough from Valleytown that they could consult a crystal ball at The World of Illusions or eat salt-water taffy without running into anyone they knew, which was important because, until she'd won her custody battle, she wanted to keep their relationship secret.

Last winter, Ted had hired Allison to replace Tammy Hudson, his first office manager, who'd embezzled over ten grand in eight months. Since then, Allison had gradually taken over his life. She plundered Ted's files of delinquent accounts, began cold-calling patients who'd assumed they'd fallen through the cracks. She ordered framed posters for the examination room ceilings. She researched prices charged by other Cherokee County dentists and convinced Ted to up his fees for extractions and root canals. She straightened his tie. She brought Ted foil-wrapped slices of pound cake, sacks of tomatoes and beans from her garden. She stayed late to finish autoclaving, and spent an entire Saturday spreading mulch in the office flowerbeds. In short, Allison made things happen. Engineered transformations. Took control. Which Ted was okay with. There were certain things it was nice not to have to worry about. Like this morning, for instance, when he'd walked from his driveway to Junaluska Road, where Allison's Maxima waited, idling on the shoulder. She'd wanted to drive; Ted claimed not to mind, as long as she let him know the minute she got tired. She said she would. She drove the whole way.

"You're wearing a sheet," Ted observed.

Allison blew a strand of hair from her mouth. She wobbled across the bed, leaped off, cried "Ta-da!" and cast the sheet aside. It ballooned with air, then drifted to the floor. Allison was now wearing a lacy black teddy, about one and a half sizes too small.

Ted flapped air into his shirt. His pits were soaked. "Whoa," he said.

"I almost got an edible one," Allison said, "but that seemed a little over the top." She ran splayed hands over her lacy bosom. Was this supposed to seduce him? Or was it a parody of self-gratification? Ted couldn't tell. He pinched a frill. It felt prickly.

"Like it?" she asked.

"Mm," he said.

Allison guided him to a bed strewn with rose petals— part of the Getaway Romance Package that included chocolate-covered strawberries and chilled champagne in a bucket. Sex with Allison—and its potent cocktail of endorphins and dopamine—had been restorative before, and this set-up, with an actual bed filling in for a dark-room or dental chair, seemed promising.

He squeezed her chunky flanks. He suckled an earlobe. A rich moan reverberated in Allison's gullet.

Ted shut his eyes.

The cabin appeared—the one he lived in now, alone. The rust streak striping the kitchen sink like blood. The shattered but still intact living room windowpane. The cabinets filled with expired soup cans, dusty rolls of toilet paper, a jar of turpentine, a box of matches, and a tube of insect-bite medicine that had burst, oozed, and dried into an unsightly clump—the cabin he and Tavey had planned to fix up. Ted would've been happy with a house in town or on a ridge overlooking the valley, but Tavey had wanted privacy. Woods. A cove at the base of a mountain. A creek. A place where their future children could build a dam, make a swimming hole, hang a rope swing—and a house they'd track dirt through when Tavey called them home to eat supper, a stew made of root vegetables from her garden. Ted could see the two of them now, renovating the old place: Tavey—in braids and a bandanna, an old T-shirt and cut-off jean shorts—reaching high to re-slather a hole with a wad of caulk, her lifted shirt exposing soft belly flesh, so that he, having no other choice, would drop what he was doing and slide a hand under her shirt. She didn't fight him off—she never did in these fantasies—and Ted imagined going straight for her neck: he could never get enough of her neck, which was long and slender with a fleshy cup at the base of the throat and a collarbone like the armature of the most wondrous musical instrument—

"Not ready?" Allison asked.

Ted folded his bottom lip under his front teeth. Too much pressure, he thought. It wasn't spontaneous. It wasn't "everybody has left the office but us." It wasn't "we've only got ten minutes." Put him back in the office during their lunch hour and he'd surely spring to life. Here, he was as limp as a wad of dough.

"Don't make that face," Allison instructed. "It's only a big deal if you decide that it is." She pressed her face against his chest, pitched a leg over his crotch, and began to writhe against his hip. "See?" she whispered. "There's more than one way to feel good."

Across the room, curtains flinched. *The air conditioner*, Ted figured, until he caught a whiff of brine. No. He'd only *thought* he'd caught a whiff of brine. Because the thing was—and this was important to remember— human beings did not come back from the dead. And those who said that they did were, he was fairly certain, not to be trusted.

Ted sucked air through his nose. He could not allow thoughts of Tavey to hijack his brain. This trip was about Allison, a woman Ted was crazy about. And, really, who wasn't? Everybody loved Allison. She was funny and big-hearted and nice. She told old ladies how pretty they looked, held the hands of first-graders getting baby teeth pulled. She knew when to be serious and when to trot out jokes: "You know you don't have to floss all your teeth, right? Just the ones you want to keep!" She noticed lost weight, manicures, perms, and new jewelry. She blessed people's hearts, swatted at people playfully when they gave her a hard time. Had something nice to say about everybody, even Donnie, her soon to be ex-husband. When patients asked how he was doing, she said, "Real good, I think he's doin' real good." Didn't say Donnie had been busted again for paraphernalia, or that he'd let Jason, their eight-year-old son, stay up until 1 a.m. watching *Terminator*. She refused to talk behind his back. That'd be mean. Anyway, her number one job now was to be a good mother. To set a good example for her child. To keep praying for his father. Because every heart, she knew, had the ability to be transformed.

"Tell me something," Ted said.

"What."

"Something new. Something you've never told me."

Allison thought for a moment. "Okay, this one time I rode a bus to Gatlinburg with my Sunday School class. We all went to Christus Gardens, you know the place with all the wax figures of Bible characters?"

Ted shook his head.

"I showed you the brochure. They've used manne-quins to recreate these scenes of the Last Supper, the Crucifixion, David and Goliath, Garden of Eden, all that. Anyway, Jesse Bailey and I were kind of together back then, and we ended up sneaking off from everybody. We made out in this like, I don't know what it was, some kind of a cave. It might've been Lazarus's Tomb. Which, if you really think about it, is kind of scary, because Jesse ended up marrying Tammy Hudson, before he married Dana."

"Weird," Ted said. He had no idea who she was talking about. He couldn't keep track of her many friends, her long history in Valleytown. He could, however, imagine a teenage Allison—braces, puffy hair, tight jeans, a gold necklace orbiting a turtleneck—because she'd set her old high school yearbook in the waiting room, and he'd checked out her Senior portrait. He could see her now, sucking face with some mulleted doof, in a cavern of faux granite, an arm's length from a mannequin wrapped in bandages.

"Your turn," Allison said.

"My turn what?"

"Tell me something."

Ted fidgeted. "I'll take a pass."

"Come on. This was your idea. Don't think. Just go."

"Okay," he said, then blurted her name: "Tavey Preston."

It'd been a long time since he'd said it aloud. Foreign and incantatory, the sound of it flooded him with panic.

Allison balanced herself on her elbows. One of the cups of her teddy had sloughed off. A nipple—like a blind eye—stared straight at him.

"Who?"

Ted cleared his throat. "Tavey Preston," he repeated. If he said it a third time, he thought, she might materialize right here in the room. "She's dead."

"Jeez. Sorry to hear that. How'd she die?"

"She was with her husband. On their honeymoon. In Mexico. She went for a swim and disappeared. Her body washed up two days later."

"Good Lord," Allison said. She ran her nails along the underside of his arm in a way that Ted figured was supposed to feel pleasurable but didn't. "That's horrible. How'd she drown?"

"Portuguese man o' war."

"Huh?"

"It's a kind of jellyfish, with tentacles that sting. Apparently, she swam into a little armada of these things."

"You can die from that?"

"If you go into anaphylactic shock, you can."

"So," Allison said. "What made you think about her?"

"I don't know. Sometimes she just kind of...appears." Ted mashed his eyelids with a forefinger and thumb. And then there she was, in the grotto of his mind. Tall and voluptuous. Long, powerful legs. Sleek arms. Green eyes. A scar on her forearm. Nearly invisible hairs on her knees. Sharp nose, with a constellation of freckles. Blonde hair pulled into a ponytail, humidity curling loose strands into ringlets. All of which inspired a familiar ache to bloom in his chest: the longing to possess physically a body that was no longer a body.

"That happens to me sometimes," Allison said. "With my Pawpaw, I mean. Only sometimes, he's actually there. Right in front of me. Like, a couple weeks ago, I looked out the kitchen window, and there he was, toting his ol' Husqvarna chainsaw through the yard. I mean, he'd always been crazy about cutting wood. I didn't know what to do. So I waved. He waved back. Then he walked into the woods. And I dunno. I guess somehow I knew he was in a better place."

"That's not the kind of feeling I get," Ted said.

Allison crawled on top of him. She squished his face in her hands. "Hey," she said. "This is Gatlinburg. We're here to party. You can mope once you get home. So starting right now," she added, "we're only gonna think about good things."

During his post-honeymoon flight back from Cozumel to JFK, Ted had swallowed a handful of Xanax then spent the majority of the trip rereading the same article in an in-flight magazine that described a chef in Chicago's meat-packing district whose dishes included sautéed lobster in Orange Crush, prosciutto cotton candy, doughnut soup, and balloons filled with flavored air—a restaurant that seemed to traffic in absurdities. He'd needed something to read, something to hold onto, because if he didn't keep his brain engaged, the grief he was trying to outrun might overtake him and summon a burning stew of bile and tears. Back then, flying back to the States with his wife's lifeless body somewhere in the cargo bay below, he figured that he might not have much more life to live, that without Tavey, he'd simply give up. But the plane landed, the days kept coming, and he found ways to survive them. Six weeks later, he drove a U-Haul from Bethesda, Maryland, to Valleytown, North Carolina, where he signed and initialed a great stack of papers that granted him a mortgage for the same decrepit cabin he and Tavey had visited months before—a structure that now seemed like a fitting embodiment of his own psychological condition—and took over the dental practice of Dr. Fred Mintz.

Only a few people in town—a mortgage broker, a realtor, and Dr. Mintz—had known that Tavey had ever existed, and when they'd asked about her, Ted had simply explained that it "hadn't worked out," a phrase that did a fine job of conveying, in vague but understandable terms, that they were no longer together. He didn't want to be defined by what he'd lost. He wanted to be known as the dentist who took his time and never hurt anybody. Then he wanted to be left alone. Better to hide Tavey inside the safety deposit box of his mind, where her memory would remain unsullied by the spectacle of revealing—again and again—the story of her demise. The only person who needed that story was Ted. It was his. *Theirs.* And, as Tavey had told him during one of her visits, no one could ever take that away.

In the bar of the Park Vista—a halved, shellacked log at the edge of the lobby that bore a hundred names and initials of its previous customers—Ted finished his first double bloody mary in three gulps and ordered another. Allison slurped a margarita, flipped through the brochures she'd gathered at a Local Attractions display, and opened one entitled *Family Jubilee!* Inside, a family of gospel singers raised sequined arms heavenward.

"Lord," Allison said. "Those outfits."

Ted's drink sparkled with sediment. To activate a shift in consciousness, he tried to imagine that Allison, bathed in the light of an ESPN special documenting the inability of the Minnesota Vikings to win a Super Bowl, was actually some kind of mythical, Scotch-Irish goddess—one who had donned modern dress to wander, undetected, among her inferiors. Her bright orange T-shirt bearing the words "Go VOLS!" was an announcement that the people of Gatlinburg could understand. It would inspire camaraderie or, barring that, good-natured enmity, among strangers she passed on the street.

"We should hurry," Allison said, slapping the brochure closed. "I made reservations at the Burning Bush."

"What," Ted replied, "no room at the Inflamed Vagina?"

Allison flicked his knee. Ted, rattling the cubes in his glass, felt vaguely heroic for making a joke. He observed the hotel balconies stacked atop one another like a layer cake, and wondered why more people, namely those with less containable impulses than his, weren't lining up to fling themselves off the top floor.

Then he saw her.

She straddled an ottoman at the center of the atrium. A greenish mist rose from her shoulders. She held a notebook at arm's length. "Tavey," she read, "you are my light. My life." She ripped out the page. It spiraled upwards. "Tavey," she read, "there is nothing in the world like our bodies knowing each other." Rip. Another page twisted up, up, and away.

"My God," Ted whispered.

"What?" Allison said.

He shook his head. Pages swirled through the air, forming a loose-leaf typhoon. "Nothing," he said. "I thought I just saw somebody."

"Who?"

"Uh," he said. His brain lurched. "Jackie Styles," he wheezed.

"Oh Lord," Allison said. "Where?" She swung her head around. Jackie Styles was a doughy, squinty-eyed woman whose hair looked as if it'd been styled during a parachute jump, a real estate agent who worked for Ralph Crisp Realty. Allison had considered Jackie a close friend until the woman agreed to testify on Donnie's behalf, during their upcoming custody case. Nothing personal, Jackie had explained, but Donnie was Jackie's second cousin. Family came first.

"No," Ted said. He touched her arm. "It wasn't her. Just my brain playing tricks on me."

Ted had been reading the letters the first time Tavey had shown up. It was late September. Twilight. A breeze wafted through the cove where he lived, and leaves, like schools of papery fish, swam through the air. Ted sat on his porch with a lantern, a box of stale American Spirits, a fat manila envelope, and a hit of ecstasy—one of two pills that Tavey's cousin Dane, a realtor from Brevard, had donated as a wedding present. He hadn't wanted to get totally wasted, so he'd broken the pill in two, thought, *what the hell*, then swallowed both halves. He opened the notebook containing the letters he and Tavey had traded back and forth during the nine months that she'd spent teaching in a private high school in Massachusetts. That night, Ted had meant to read them one last time, by fire-light, then set them ablaze.

He was three-quarters through the notebook when a green light appeared at the far end of the meadow. *Foxfire*, he'd thought. The light grew brighter. Expanded. Morphed into a figure. No big deal. The ecstasy, he figured, was in full force. And he'd overdosed on the words of his dead wife. The notebook paper was velvety and alive with traces of her perfume. It was all merely an elaborate hallucination. Nothing to fear.

"What time is it?" she asked.

"Late," Ted replied.

She nodded, shivering.

"You cold?" he asked.

"No," she replied. She stroked a forearm. Liquid oozed from a wound. It looked like light. Fluid—a luminous, self-replenishing secretion—streamed over her body. "Something's wrong with me," she said, rubbing her arms. "I can't dry off."

So, Ted thought. She doesn't know. And he didn't have the heart to tell her.

"Want a drink?" he asked.

She didn't answer. He poured an inch of bourbon into a glass and set it on the porch railing. She ignored it. "I had this horrible dream," she said.

"Oh," Ted said.

"I know you don't like to hear me tell them," she replied.

"No," he said, "it's okay."

Her lips quivered. "This one was *awful*. We were in Mexico. In a pool. You wouldn't talk to me. You kept swimming away. Toward some other woman. She was laughing at me. I kept calling your name, but you wouldn't answer."

"Hey," Ted said. He had reached out a hand. She stepped back. "Here," he said. "Listen." Then he had read aloud a paragraph she'd written about how much she was looking forward to moving to the cabin, how she'd had a dream where the trout in their pond were so friendly that they could catch them with their hands, pet their glistening scales before sending them off again to shimmy into the murk. It hadn't taken long to read. It was only a few lines. But when Ted glanced up from the page, no one was there.

The Burning Bush promised to be a success. The hostess, Jamie, a teenager with braces and green hair guided them to window seats overlooking the parking lot, where half a dozen middle-aged couples, having dismounted Harleys, were shedding their leather. Jamie pulled a trigger on a grill lighter and ignited their votive.

"Nice," Ted said. Despite the relative darkness and candlelight, which made it possible to imagine that each table might, at any moment, conduct its own private séance, the dining room, filled as it was with people, most of whom were overweight and quite jolly, seemed apparition-free: a dim sanctuary where Ted and Allison could peacefully feast.

"Well, this beats riding to the cabin on the floor mat of your Lariat," Allison observed.

"Indeed." A few weeks ago, Ted had picked up Allison in the parking lot of Hardee's, then bounded down the streets of Valleytown with her slumped on the floor of the truck, to ensure nobody in town would spot them riding together. The visit hadn't lasted long. Ted had only just flipped the steaks—the two best slabs of filet from Ingle's—when Allison received a call: Jason's dad had forgotten to pick him up from baseball practice. They'd have to call it a night.

Allison frowned. "What are you getting?"

"I dunno," Ted said. "The cowboy rib-eye?" He felt a twinge in his gut, remembered the onesie he'd seen in the window of the Smoky Mountain Gift Shoppe, the one that had said, "This Isn't a Milk Belly, It's a Fuel Tank for a Poo Poo Machine!" It had reminded him about how one of his patients—the old guy from the health food store who'd left Ted a jar full of barley grass juice powder—had explained that babies, with their squeaky-clean intestinal tracts, pooped upwards of three times a day—sometimes six, depending upon how many meals they ate—while the average American, guts clogged with indigestible fat-curds, took a dump only three times a week. Maybe, Ted thought, he should ditch the rib-eye in favor of the spinach salad with grilled chicken. He folded his menu. Noticed that Tavey was standing outside the window. Her body radiated a pale, bioluminescent glow. A halo of moths orbited—but never lighted upon—her head. He was sure he could hear the sound of their wings: like a theremin on fast-forward.

•

"Where's your friend?" Tavey asked. She had passed through the window as if it were a sheet of still water, and now, in the candlelight, her wet flesh shimmered. A laceration opened and closed in her arm, like a gruesome mouth trying to breathe.

"Bathroom," Ted said.

"Freshening up for you?"

"Don't get the wrong idea."

"You're having dinner with another woman. What am I supposed to think?"

"She's a friend," Ted said. Heat rose in his throat, activated the part of his brain that stored the memory of when he and Allison—the only ones left in the office— had first retreated to the darkroom, where, by the faint light of the red power button on the X-ray machine, they'd engaged in an impromptu grope-session. *We may be moving too fast*, Ted had whispered. *We'll go as slow as you want*, Allison had replied. And then they'd sped up.

Tavey slid a hand around Ted's arm. An electric current zapped his funny bone. "Sorry," she said. "I don't like being forgotten."

"Impossible."

"You still love me?"

"Please."

"Then come back with me. We'll start over. We'll pretend none of this ever happened."

"But it did," Ted whispered. "It *did* happen."

"Room 1001," she said. "I'll be waiting."

One thousand one. The number had been burned onto a wooden slat above the door to their room in Mexico, the place where Ted had, in between trips to the bathroom, wallowed, searching the pebbled ceiling for encouragement as he tried to understand the idea of having sworn himself, for all eternity, to a woman he'd known for less than a year. He'd worried that he didn't love her enough; he'd worried that he loved her too much or for the wrong reasons. He'd worried what it portended when a man got sick on his honeymoon. He'd worried, for the most part, about being a failure.

On the morning of the fourth day of the trip, Tavey returned from the pool smelling of coconut and tequila. Ted grunted. She sat on the edge of the bed and began to smooth his hair.

"You're turning a corner," Tavey said. "I can feel it."

"I'm disgusting," Ted replied.

"You're not disgusting. You're my husband."

"Fine then. I'm a disgusting husband."

"Only some of the time." Tavey smiled. Ted pressed his nose to her head. Her scalp smelled like scalp. Tavey used scentless shampoo, eschewed deodorant. She wasn't crazy about the idea of aluminum seeping into her lymph nodes.

"Should you take something else?" Tavey said.

"I've taken everything there is."

"Then just lie here with me and think nice thoughts."

"We should've gone to Sweden," he whispered.

"No negatives," Tavey said. "Unless you double up."

"Shit." Ted placed a hand on his abdomen.

"You need to go?"

"Maybe."

"Poor baby."

"I'm not getting better."

"You will."

"I can't get much worse."

"I love you," Tavey said.

"No you don't," Ted replied. He knew—as soon as he'd said it—that it was a stupid thing to say. It wasn't that he didn't believe her; he only wanted to indulge his infantile need for her to tell him she loved him again.

"I don't like that," Tavey said. She thrust a finger into his face. "That's not nice. Even joking."

She slid into flip-flops, yanked a drying towel from a chair.

"Hey," Ted said. "I'm sorry. I'm sick."

"I know you're sick. Trust me. If there's one thing I know, it's that *you* are *sick*."

"See! You do resent it."

"Ted, please! Things could be worse. A lot worse."

"Where are you going?"

"To the beach."

"I'll go with you."

"No, you won't."

"Yes. I can do it. I want to."

"But I don't want you to."

"Come on, Tavey."

"Don't push it," she said. Her eyes narrowed. Nostrils flared. She jerked the curtains open. Beyond the sliding door, sprinklers cast mist into the air, glazing green lawns. Beyond the grass: the blinding white beach sand. Beyond that: the ocean, with its a gazillion shimmering knife-blades of light. Ted watched from the patio as Tavey flip-flopped through the grass, kicked through the sand. She peeled off her shirt, dropped it and her towel in a heap, then sloshed into the water, dived in. Her body diminished, melted to a tiny bobbing dot, then disappeared from his field of vision.

"You don't have Jagermeister?" Allison yelled. She had passed buzzed an hour before and was on her way to drunk. A cowboy hat sat cockeyed on the back of her swiveling head. Ted had no idea where she'd gotten it. "I thought this was a biker bar!"

The goateed bartender, who was pouring body shots into the bellybuttons of a couple of moms who were letting their hair down, ignored her.

"They have Sambuca," Ted noted.

"Jagermeister!" Allison yelled.

"I need to tell you something!" Ted said. He finished the rest of his vodka tonic; ice clattered into his face and down his shirt. "It's sort of a big deal."

"Don't tell me," Allison said. She swatted at his shirt, to knock off the cubes. "You've been cheating on me with Jackie Styles."

Ted winced. "It's a little worse than that."

She cocked her wobbling head. Slitted her eyes. "Not Mandy Hogsed. Please don't say Mandy Hogsed."

"I had a wife," he said.

Allison's nose wrinkled, as if she'd just smelled something foul. "You had a what?"

"A wife," Ted repeated. "I was married."

Allison shoved him; he nearly fell off the stool. "Get out!"

"No," he said. "I'm serious."

"Who?"

"Tavey," Ted said. "Tavey Preston."

"Wait," Allison said. "You mean . . . your friend? The one who . . ."

"Yeah," Ted said. "Before I started my practice. I met her at a Christmas party. We hit it off. Three months later, we agreed we couldn't live without each other."

Allison moved closer. Ted glanced into the mirror as a way to scan the room. Tavey wasn't there, so he continued the story. The long distance courtship. The engagement via email. The wedding. The honeymoon. Ted's sickness. Tavey's death.

"Wow," Allison said. "You're a mess."

"I know."

"I bet you think you'll never love somebody as much as her."

"I don't think I will."

"Probably not," Allison said. "I'm so sorry."

"There's more."

"I'm sure there is."

"Sometimes . . . like in the darkroom?" He was parched. He tipped his drink back. A mere droplet dribbled into his mouth.

"Spit it out."

"I pretended you were her."

Ted blinked. He'd imagined this confession would disgust Allison, that she might respond with a slap, or at least a jaw-dropping expression of shock. But she remained surprisingly silent and composed. Her bottom lip quivered, her eyes grew watery, and she ran a hand through his hair, an event that Ted found profoundly disappointing: he had hoped she would've found some way to punish him. Instead, she laced an arm around his, whispered something he couldn't understand in his ear, and tugged him away.

In their room at the Park Vista, Allison instructed Ted to remove his clothes; she was going to make love to him. Ted unbuttoned his shirt. Slid off his pants. Excused himself. Visited the bathroom. Brushed his teeth. Avoided his reflection. Returned to bed, where Allison commanded him to lie down. She drunkenly shucked his jeans, then climbed on top of him, and whispered hotly into his ear: "It's okay to pretend." She pulled back the waistband of his boxers. Ted shut his eyes, felt her mouth engulf him. But he couldn't pretend. He could see straight through his shut lids, where, despite Allison's efforts, not much was happening.

"Hey," he whispered.

Allison lifted her head. She looked dazed. As if she'd gone somewhere else in her mind. "Yeah?"

"I may need to . . . visit the bathroom one more time."

"Okay," she said. "But hurry."

Ted didn't hurry. He sat on the toilet, waited, then flushed, took his time washing he hands. When he returned, Allison was curled in a fetal position on the bed, her hands folded under her head like a sleeping child. Ted lay down beside her, turned on the TV. Arthur, the rich drunk, was taking a bath in his top hat. Ted waited for the song about the moon and New York City, then zapped it off. Allison snorted, rolled over. He told himself he would not get out of bed. He would not leave the room. He would not look for Room 1001. For hours, he congratulated himself on staying put—on not going, on continuing not to go. He tried to imagine a future when he would look back on this moment and praise his steadfastness. Instead, he ended up thinking about the past, which was often what happened when he closed his eyes. In his imagination, he flung himself through space and time to an all-inclusive resort in sun-blasted Mexico.

He couldn't find his wife. She wasn't at the pool. She wasn't in the main lobby. She wasn't in the mangrove swamp. She wasn't at Mayan Ruins—a pyramid-shaped drink stand operated by a lone bartender who poured green slush into a cup emblazoned with the face of a sun god.

He shuffled into one of the resort's open-air snack bars, twisting the plastic bracelet he'd been wearing on his wrist since check-in, the one that made him feel like a hospital patient out for a walk and which identified him as a guest who'd failed to shell out the extra five hundred bucks it would've taken in order to be welcomed at one of the adjacent hotels—or, for that matter, to take a walk more than two hundred yards in either direction on the beach. Not that it mattered. The Snack Hut was as far as he had wandered in days. Already, he was exhausted.

He slid a bottle of antacid from a pocket in his cargo shorts. Between sips, he scanned the horde of sand-encrusted tourists milling beneath the thatched roof. A woman with spiky blonde hair and a cigarette dangling from her mouth carried a paper boat of nachos in one hand, chili fries in another. A man in a Speedo vigorously sawed a slice of pizza with a bendy knife, his breasts shimmying as he carved.

He frowned. Not a single person here was his wife. It seemed wrong; a man on his honeymoon should never be in the position of not knowing where his wife was, much less hoping the generic Pepto he'd just chugged would extinguish the volcanic activity in his lower intestines. Maybe, he thought, he was getting what he deserved. Maybe the illness was a sign. Maybe he hadn't been poisoned by Mexican water or bacteria spores floating in on trade winds or the ham sandwich he'd devoured on the flight from Atlanta. Maybe this virus, this infection, this evil spirit was a manifestation of the terror that'd gripped him three days before, when he'd stood at the front of a church and solemnly pledged himself, for all eternity, to one woman. If one were to think about these vows in the abstract, and he had, they suggested a rather ominous finality. *Last. Only. Forevermore.* There were no more *maybes.* No more *mights.* Tavey was it. He wanted not to feel trapped by committing to the love of his life. But the word *forever* made his chest feel tight. Like he might be running out of air.

Ted woke up sweaty. He peeled the sheet away, rolled off the bed, gathered his clothes. The prong of his belt buckle clinked. He grimaced. Dressed quietly. Opened the door. Exited.

Room 1001 should've been easy enough to find—either to the left of 1002 or to the right. It was in neither place. Ted orbited the tenth level—again and again. The aroma of coffee and french toast sticks drifted up from the atrium. It was morning. Ted found every number from 1002 to 1038, but no 1001. He walked around again. Nada. Finally, after his third trip, it appeared. A door in a place where a door hadn't been. Ted squinted. Zeros merged. The room number transformed itself. Two single digits, separated by infinity.

The door had been left open. Just a crack. Ted nudged it with his foot. "Hello?" he said. He entered. Nothing. He flipped a light switch. Nothing. He clicked the door shut, jogged to the window and nearly fell. The floor—it wasn't carpet, more like marble—was slick, as if it'd just been mopped.

He drew back the shades. Darkness melted; the room took shape. He rubbed his arms: it was freezing. He twisted a dial on the A/C. The unit rattled on. Two fat, black suitcases sat in the corner. Coincidence, he thought, lifting one of the floppy lids. But, no. The Ray Bans, the floral print tank tops, the red bikini, the capri pants, the scarves—they were all Tavey's. The clothes were ice-cold, as if they'd spent the last two years in deep freeze. The fabric stung his hands, but Ted kept burrowing, as if he might reach the throbbing center of this dream and switch it off. Instead, he unearthed a pair of pink, frosty briefs. He pressed them against his cheeks.

He didn't hear the key turning in the lock, never heard the door creak open—only the slap and suck of bare feet against wet stone. She was beside him. Greenish fluid slithered over her body. A sliver of fin peeled itself from her elbow and drifted onto the floor.

Ted had dreamed dreams like this. Dreams where he'd entered a church, a package store, the cabin and found a door that, when opened, revealed a corridor leading to this room. He'd indulged waking fantasies, too: episodes in which the flashes of Tavey's face in a passing car or what looked like her body in the distance gave rise to hopes that perhaps she was still alive and had, after years of searching, found her way back. This Tavey, though, unlike those others, refused to dissolve. She radiated.

"I thought something happened to you," she said. She picked absentmindedly at a piece of shell on her forearm.

"Something has," Ted said.

"You look terrible."

"Actually," Ted replied, "I don't feel so hot."

"Vacations always make you sick," Tavey said, shaking her head. She tugged a strand of seaweed from her hair, then slung it against the wall, where it stuck in the shape of an S.

"Listen," Ted said. "I need you to know something."

"Okay."

"That woman you saw? I told her. About us."

"Everything?"

"Yes."

"Even . . ."

"Yes. I told her that you'd come back."

She turned her back to him. A series of scratches pulsed like breathing embers. "You want me to die again, don't you?"

"No."

"Yes, you do. You want me out of your life."

"No," Ted said. "No. Please. Tavey. Come here."

Ted knew that love and the making of it was supposed to be reserved for the living. But somehow she was here, and he needed to hold her, to feel her body against his: one flesh, eternal conspirators in this life on Earth.

He could have predicted the cold. The wet, sandy grit. The teeth-like shells biting into his skin. He wouldn't have been shocked if her flesh had fallen away in chunks, revealing brittle, crumbling bones. But she remained intact. Her thighs, plastered with grime, scraped against his until he couldn't feel his legs. She slid her tongue into his mouth. His teeth froze. Each frigid lick erased a band of sensation in his lips. The numbness spread into his face. Colonized his head. His vision blurred. Went dark. Her breasts—grainy, chilled globes of flesh— squished against his chest, the nipples stabbing him like tiny stones of ice. His pulse slowed. Suffocation, he felt, was imminent. He thrust the last feeling part of himself inside her, and then he was gone.

Ted woke to cold tile. Allison loomed above, brushing her teeth. She wore a pair of his boxers, but nothing else. Her arm vibrated vigorously. Her breasts, bare, wobbled.

"Good morning there, Mr. Wild Man!" she exclaimed, pausing to spit a thick string of toothpaste into the sink.

"How'd I get here?"

"Hell if I know," she said. "I haven't the foggiest idea of how we got back to the hotel. But I had the craziest dreams."

"Huh."

"Yeah, there were all these locusts or crickets or something. Swarming all over me. I'm surprised I didn't barf in my sleep. You hungry?"

Ted repressed a grimace. His stomach was churning. Like something inside wanted out.

Ye Old Pancake House resembled a cabin of intersecting notched logs, the kind made famous by westward-heading American pioneers. On its roof, a pair of droopy-eyed, animatronic bears took swigs from jugs branded with triple Xs. Inside, Ted and Allison studied bright paper menus that doubled as placemats. Allison ordered the Lumberjack Special: flapjacks, scrambled eggs, sausage, bacon, hash browns, toast. Ted requested black coffee and a fruit cup.

"You know," Allison said, "I really admire you."

"Well, I'm glad to hear that," Ted replied. "It's not every day you find a naked man passed out on a bathroom floor."

"Seriously," she said, dunking a sausage link in a tub of syrup, "I can't get over it. How hard it must have been after she died. A whole life, gone."

"Pretty much," Ted said. His couldn't taste his coffee; the same effect might've been achieved by swirling a tablespoon of soil into tepid water.

"You must think about her a lot."

Ted shrugged. "She comes and goes."

Allison stabbed a slab of pancake. "It's just so hard to imagine."

"It's easier than you think," Ted said. His speared a withered sausage link at the edge of Allison's plate, shoved the whole thing into his mouth. "Especially if you keep moving. You sit around too long by yourself, that's when it catches up with you—"

"But come on, Ted. Your wife didn't just die. She *drowned*. On your freaking *honeymoon*. That's like, I don't know, the worst thing I've ever heard?"

"They say drowning's one of the best ways to go."

"I'm talking about you," Allison said. One of Allison's sock feet found Ted's crotch, began generously kneading.

"I'm fine."

"How so?" Allison said. Her foot's stroking had resulted in an unexpected tumescence. Was she employing her toe knuckles?

"You know," he wheezed. "Just trying to live in the here and now."

"Ah," she said. "Sort of like seize the day or whatever."

"Sure."

Allison grinned. "I know something I'd like to seize."

Ted raised an eyebrow. "Oh yeah?"

"Yeah." Allison shook the watch on her wrist. Counted on her fingers. "We have plenty of time."

"We do?"

"Yup. At least seven hours before Donnie drops Jason off at the house."

Ted set his fork down. "Then what are we waiting for?"

"Ha. You can say that now, now that we've checked out of the hotel."

"We'll just get another room. I'm a rich dentist, remember?"

"I have a better idea," Allison said. She shouldered her pocketbook, unleashed a mischievous grin. Then she whispered in Ted's ear: "You wanna do something *crazy*?"

Ted did not want to do something crazy. He wanted to do the least crazy thing possible: he wanted to get into Allison's Maxima and go home. Not his home. Hers. He'd never been there. Allison had talked about sneaking him over for wine and baked spaghetti, but it hadn't worked out. Her place, Ted was sure, would offer a treasury of symbols assuring anyone who entered that the house was lived in and loved: recliners with ribbed fabric and plastic cup holders, a clock made from lacquered slab of wood on the wall, dying plants, a stained glass lamp over the breakfast nook, carpet whose every stain had a story. There'd be a box of forgotten Marlboro Lights in the back of the kitchen junk drawer, fish sticks in the freezer, a faded Tennessee Vols sticker in the corner of the bathroom mirror, and a medicine cabinet filled with expired drugs that Ted could plunder after he and Allison rode the undulations of her waterbed, where they would—if he had anything to say about it—remain indefinitely.

They exited the front doors of Ye Old Pancake House

and descended the rough-hewn stairs, cut through a yard strewn with energy drink cans, cigarette boxes, Skoal tins, and a diaper. They ran across four lanes of traffic, and crossed a vast parking lot, where, upon reaching the shores of an orange-roofed strip mall, they entered a Liz Claiborne outlet. On the first floor, right near the door, was Women's Accessories.

"Act like you're shopping," Allison whispered. "You know. Look at stuff. No, goober. Not here. In the men's section. Over there."

"Right," Ted said.

"In five minutes, I'll meet you in one of the changing rooms."

"How will you know it's me?"

"Leave your shoes on," she whispered.

In the changing room, someone had Sharpied a pentagram onto the wall. Ted hung the clothes he'd gathered on a hook. He performed some stretches. Shadowboxed. He wanted to check his reflection, but there was no mirror. He felt his face. His hair.

"Ted," a voice whispered.

On the floor, a puddle seeped mercurially across the carpet. It was coming from next door.

"Tavey?"

She crawled under. Ted smiled. Yes, her flesh glittered with grit and she reeked of brine and her hair was still laced with seaweed, but she looked, well, more *alive*. Her wounds weren't weeping.

He licked her neck. *One last time*, he thought. He would touch and hold the woman he loved. God, she was cold. His lips buzzed with numbness. He fumbled with the strings of her bathing suit top. Her flesh scorched his fingertips.

"Wait," Tavey said.

"What's wrong?" Ted couldn't feel his face. Or, for that matter, his head. The sensation was not unlike treating himself to two 7.5 milligram pills of hydrocodone, tiny packets of which arrived in a sampler box courtesy of Abbot Labs, delivered by Fed Ex straight to his office door.

Tavey patted her stomach. "I'm worried."

"About what?"

"I can't remember the last time the baby moved."

"Baby?"

"Sorry," she said. "I can't remember the last time *he* moved."

"Hold up," Ted said. "You're not making sense."

"The baby. *Our* baby."

"But we never made a baby together."

"I'm not in the mood for jokes."

"I wasn't trying to be funny."

"Ted?" It was Allison. Ted recognized her Keds peeking under the door. "You okay in there?"

"Not her again," Tavey said.

"Come in," Ted said.

"The door's locked," Allison whispered.

"Just a second," Ted replied.

"Hurry," Allison whispered.

"Need some help?" a sales girl asked.

"We're fine," Allison said. She threw a pair of brown slacks over the top of the door. "So, uh, I guess you could try these on when you get a chance, hon. I think they'd look really nice with that plaid shirt."

"You gotta hide," Ted whispered.

"Do what?" Allison asked.

"Uh, nothing!" Ted said.

"Open your mouth," Tavey instructed.

"Why?"

"Just do it."

Ted did it.

"Wider," she said. She slid a finger inside. Then her entire hand.

"A little wider," she said. It was something Ted said to his patients every day. Something he understood. And so, he obeyed. He opened wide. Her arm—like a slushy gelatin of frozen coals—wormed its way down his throat. Once Tavey's arm had slithered into his chest, her hand grabbed hold of his heart, and, using that palpitating muscle as a kind of anchor, she hauled the rest of herself inside him. The whole thing was over in seconds.

Ted gurgled. Burped. Took stock of himself. He felt pretty okay. A little tingly. Very awake. Maybe, he told himself, this was the solution: they'd simply have to share one body. Which, now that he thought about it, didn't feel so bad. Sure, he'd lost sensation in his arms and legs, and yes, he felt a bit denser, as if his internal organs had taken on weight, or were beginning to congeal, but he wasn't scared. He flipped the lock. Pushed open the door. And, as he exited the changing room and strolled past Allison, nearly toppling a rack promising fifty percent off, he felt a sense of relief wash over him. He was no longer telling his body what to do. It was doing what it was doing on its own.

As he passed through the front door, the tags on the pants he was wearing—and had not paid for—were zapped by invisible rays, and an alarm began to bleat, summoning a prune-faced gal in a silky shirt. She wrung her gnarled hands. Ted explained: he hadn't come for the pants; he and his office manager were just going to use one of the changing rooms as a fuck booth. He unzipped the pants, folded them over his arm, and handed them to the woman. Then he walked out of the store, wearing briefs.

"Ted," Allison said, "what are you doing?"

Ted glanced down at his legs—white, skinny, with

whorls of brown hair. "It could be worse," he said. "I could
be wearing a teddy."

Ted was not opposed to offering an explanation. Explanations, he knew, had the power to re-make the world. But
explanations required one to be able to use one's body,
and that, at this time, was not possible, which was too
bad, since, after they'd left Gatlinburg behind, and had
been driving up, up, up, winding around and around and
around, he would've liked to open his window to get some
air. Unfortunately, he could not work his arms. That is,
they moved and twitched and crossed and uncrossed
themselves, but not of his own accord. Also, he seemed
to be seeing things. The leaves, for instance. They'd
been so green in the valley, but now they were dappled
red. Actually, they were bleeding. That was interesting.
Because as far as he knew, leaves didn't bleed.

   Ted's mouth opened. And this came out: "So, was it
good for you?"

   Allison shook her head and smiled. It was not, however, the kind of smile that expressed amusement. She
looked sort of pissed.

   "You know," he said, "you really should think about fix-
ing that overbite."

   "I know what you're doing," she said. "You're trying to
hurt me."

   "Trust me," the mouth said. "If I wanted to hurt you, I
wouldn't have to try."

   Ted clamped his lips shut. His knees whapped
together. His original plan, after Tavey'd gone in, was to
let the whole possession thing take its course. But now,
it seemed, some action would have to be taken. Only he
wasn't exactly sure what.

   "I understand, though," Allison said. "It's all about
guilt. You're feeling guilty."

Ted wheezed. He felt a pressure in his belly. A silent rumbling.

"You know," she said, "you're not the only one who's ever had to deal with loss. It's not like you have, like, some kind of . . . I don't know the word."

"Exclusive rights?" Ted asked.

"Whatever. I just mean you're not the only one who's ever loved someone." The radio was fizzling out. Allison shoved a cassette into the mouth of the tape deck. An old timey gospel quartet began to sing. Awful voices harmonized; it sounded like old men straining to sing through their noses.

"But wait," Ted said. "I never loved you.

Allison's fists tightened on the wheel. "Nobody said—"

"In fact, I could never . . . love a woman like you."

"Nobody said you had to."

"I just needed someone . . . I just needed . . . a body."

Allison wiped her eyes. A black rivulet of mascara ran alongside her nose. She smeared it around with a thumb. "Well," she said, "I'm glad I could be of service."

Ted tried to apologize, but emitted only a wheeze. He didn't know how to explain. These weren't his words. Not exactly. He wasn't in control. And his guts! They were boiling.

"What is it?"

"Please," Ted managed. "Stop."

"Fine," Allison replied. "Be like that. I won't even—"

"No," he said. "The car. *Please stop the car.*"

Ted was lucky. For miles, there'd been nothing but trees and guardrails and the back end of a Plymouth Voyager whose rear window indicated—thanks to the family of zombies that'd been plastered to its window—that the vehicle belonged to a family of four. Now, thank God, a sign declared SCENIC VIEW. Allison swerved into the lot.

Ted flung the door open. His stomach burbled. It felt to him like something inside was attempting various points of exit. He stumbled outside, ignoring Allison's inquiries about what was wrong with him, imagining that maybe, despite everything he knew about science and religion and gastronomy, that something, not a baby, surely, but some *thing*, had indeed transpired in the belly of his dead wife and that this might actually be something to worry about, since whatever was in there was the product of the living mingling with the non-living, and because you couldn't just sleep with your dead wife without avoiding serious repercussion, he understood that now, but he also understood that there was no way that he could've *not* slept with her, because no matter how much he wanted to deny it, he missed her, and he was glad, happy even, that she had chosen to enter his body, and oh! There it was again, the sharp pain in his midsection, like claws practicing a staccato tarantella on his duodenum. He scanned the parking lot for a little sign with a man on it, because he wanted to believe that maybe the churning in his gut was nothing more than an overdue bowel move-ment, but he found no restroom, no hovel, no hut where he could squat and expel his load. He had no choice, then. Into the woods. He ran, clutching his stomach, along a path canopied with fluttering green leaves. Allison yelled, "Where are you going?" and he yelled back, unconvinc-ingly, "Nowhere!" The path he traveled was veined with roots, and he tripped—losing his balance—a few times. A cold rain fell; he could feel every prick. Ahead, he could see that the path ended, and at the end sat a rock, like a giant shoulder blade, covered in crunchy, incandescent fungi. He climbed aboard.

"Beautiful, isn't it?" A bald man, with a stripe of greasy hair that'd been slapped halfway across his dome, wrin-kled his nose at Ted. He tapped his walking stick against the rock. He was missing a bicuspid. "I'd say this was worth the trip, wouldn't you?" In the distance, the tip of a mountain appeared, a soft, plum-colored island rising from an ocean of fog. It occurred to Ted that if someone could stay afloat in that murk, they might be able to swim across.

"It's time," Tavey said.

"Time?" Ted replied. "For what?"

"The time?" the old man asked. He glanced at a watchless wrist, then into the clouds above. "I'd say it's about noon."

Ted doubled over. "Oh!" he gasped.

"You okay?"

"No," he groaned.

"He's coming," Tavey moaned.

"Should I call 911?"

"Who's coming?" Ted yelled. "Who the fuck is coming?"

"Looks like a woman to me," the old man said, peering down the trail. "Red hair. Average height. Appears to be on the voluptuous side of things."

Ted slipped his hand under his shirt. The flesh of his stomach felt slick. He was afraid to look. Using his fingertips, he traced the fluid-trail to his navel. It didn't seem possible. The little fleshy bulb—his outie!—was nowhere to be found. In its place, a dime-sized opening. He was leaking. He had no desire to probe the hole, but his finger had a mind of its own. In it went. There, he felt something else, no bigger than a nodule, slimy and hard. It had length, Ted discovered: a tiny, jointed bone-thing, a finger-shaped-thing connected to other finger-shaped-things, which formed a tiny, bony hand-thing, a fleshless baby hand, which now gripped one of Ted's own fingers.

"Wait!" Allison said.

Ted coughed-barfed bile. Instinctively, he drew his right hand back, to wipe his chin. The little hand wouldn't let go of the finger.

"Ted!" Allison shouted. "Please! I can't go down there!"

Ted couldn't blame her. Down here was pretty scary. There was wind, for one thing. And rain, which was making the rock pretty slick. And the ledge. Over which he now peered, into the churning sea of cloud, a river of mist.

Ted had hoped that his life would never, under any circumstances, flash before his eyes. The idea that a person could revisit the past was, of course, a seductively dangerous fiction: once the present had perished, there was no bringing it back.

"You're being ridiculous," Tavey said. "You can't save a person like that. I mean, look at her."

Ted shook his head. He would not look. If Allison was on her knees, crawling down the rock, or scooting toward him on her behind, he didn't want to know.

"She's better than you think," he whispered.

"Better than me?"

He shook his head. It wasn't about who was better. Or whom he really loved. Tavey knew that. But poor Allison! She'd given it her all. And she believed in people. In their essential goodness, in their ability to change, in—

"It doesn't matter what she believes," Tavey said. "You're with us now. We're a family."

Ted guessed she was right. The little hand—so strong! so insistent!—wouldn't stop tugging Ted's finger, urging him ever onward. Except there wasn't much onward left. There was the rock—a kind of downward-sloping ramp, carved by ice and wind and snow, ready for someone, namely Ted, to finally use it as a launching pad into the great maw of the unknown. One more step, then: into the clouds. He grimaced, waiting for his head to unleash the terrifying movie of his life, waiting for his heart to pump some paralyzing remorse through his body, waiting for Tavey to laugh or cry or cheer or boo. But Tavey didn't say anything. She was making a some kind of sound—a faint, off-key hum, like a mirthless lullaby—but she spoke not a word, not even his name. There was no name for him now, no name for where he was going. There was only the wind and the rain lashing his face—that and the little baby hand, its tiny bones sweetly squeezing his finger, reminding him, by not letting go, that this was not, no matter what he might like to believe, the end.

Probation

➤➤ ◀◀

ABE STROKES THE REDIAL button with his thumb. One more minute and he'll call again. Not that calling will help. He's pretty sure the battery in his wife's phone has died. He stopped leaving messages half an hour ago, but keeps calling on the off chance that she's plugged in her charger. With any luck, she won't see how many calls originated from his phone and think he's gone slam crazy. Though maybe he has. Gone slam crazy. Is it crazy, after waiting three hours for your twelve-year-old daughter to come home, to close your eyes and see crushed skulls and blood and semen and shallow graves and basements converted into dungeons? He doesn't know. This showing up late business is new.

Abe presses ON. Then REDIAL. Once again: voice mail.

"Where the hell's your mother?" Abe asks Tommy, his ten-year-old. He slams the phone on the coffee table. The lid pops off. The battery falls out.

"She's always letting her phone die," Tommy says.

Tommy's watching a show about people rescuing dogs from people who've rescued too many dogs.

"Why even have it if you don't keep it charged?" Abe says.

"Maybe she doesn't feel like talking."

"Shit," Abe says. "I don't feel like talking and I keep mine charged."

"Guess you should get me and Alex some phones of our own."

"And how would I pay for 'em? With my good looks?"

"Just saying," Tommy says.

On the TV, an ASPCA official pets an emaciated dog. Every bone in its body shows. Its tail wags. Tommy aims the remote and fires.

A week and a half ago, Abe got a call from Bob Trueblood, principal of Valleytown Elementary. Trueblood wanted to talk to Abe about the sixth-grade field trip to Health Adventure, a place in nearby Asheville that Abe had also visited as a middle-schooler and that he remembers as a kind of underground museum with giant foam body parts and a big plastic heart with stairs inside and where a talking skeleton teaches viewers to appreciate the cooperation of a person's bones by pedaling a stationary bicycle.

"Turns out," Trueblood said, "on the ride back, Alex and a boy, well, there's no way of putting this delicately. Apparently the boy dared Alex to *lick* him."

"Lick," Abe repeated.

"To put it bluntly," Trueblood replied, "I think we're talking oral sex here."

Impossible, Abe thought. His baby girl? Did anyone even know what a blow job was at twelve? He sure hadn't. Had he? Okay, so he probably had an idea, but he hadn't come anywhere close to *getting* one. At that age, a blow job was about as likely as Cindy Crawford climbing out of *Sports Illustrated* in a mesh bathing suit and asking if he felt like taking a shower. It wasn't even until he was Alex's age or maybe even a little older that he'd spent the night at Jeremy Small's house, where he'd watched, on an unscrambled satellite feed, his first R-rated movie, *The Joy of Sex*, though the only thing he remembers from that particular film, aside from a couple of titty scenes (which, thanks to their brief duration, proved unsatisfying, even after they rewound and tried to pause them, since the poor tracking emblazoned every bare chest with lines of white snow), is a kid rolling up a giant towel and dangling it at crotch level and yelling "Moby Dick!" This joke, which had once struck Abe as hilariously perverted, now seems comparatively wholesome when faced with the trannies, midgets, and the strip-teasing morbidly obese of regular daytime TV. Add this to the fact that the entire town has been talking about the videotape of Alex's mother straddling a sixty-year-old man in the employee break room of Ingle's grocery and you have more than enough material to suggest to an impressionable girl that putting her mouth on some kid's nasty little dingle is an okay thing to do.

Abe stuffs the phone into the pocket of his work shirt, which is awkward, since three-fourths of it sticks out, but he leaves it there. The shirt says, "Abe" on one side and "Shell" on the other. It's grease-smudged. Itchy. He'd like to change into something more comfortable. In less than twelve hours he'll have to put it back on again. But he doesn't change. He opens the front door.

"Where do you think *you're* going?" Tommy says.

"Nowhere," Abe says.

"Don't let Mashburn see you."

Abe steps onto the porch. The door slams behind him. It's warm for October. Rainy. A car glides past, tires sizzling across the pavement.

"I ain't worried about Mashburn," Abe whispers, as if saying it might make it true.

Abe's not supposed to leave the house unless he's headed to the Quick Lube—straight there and back, no detours or stop-offs. This is one of the rules of his probation—that and no drinking, no firearms. He's been pretty good; aside from a Bud Lite now and then (which he drinks from an O'Doul's can, in case his probation officer shows up), he's fought off every other temptation: the idea of a Sunday afternoon fishing the deep, spectral holes of Beaver Creek; an inexplicable desire to rent the movie *Predator;* a midnight walk up the hill to the elementary school soccer field, where, standing upon turf mushed by cleats, he might look down upon the house where he was born and where his mother died, where a lone bulb in the kitchen would be shining like a beacon, inspiring solemn thoughts about his kids asleep in their beds. Fortunately, entertaining such excursion fantasies has required Abe to also imagine what it'd be like to run into somebody he knows, or only sort of knows, somebody who'd say something like, "They finally let you out of the house?" or "Look who's been re-introduced to civilization"—after which he'd ask Abe to recount the whole chopper story, which Abe's sick of telling but has tried his best to own up to, since, honestly, if he'd heard a story about a bunch of ATF guys in ninja suits beating the snot out of some dude after he'd shone a toy laser at an FBI helicopter, he'd ask for details, too. Only he'd hope that eventually he'd have the sense to let up, give the guy a break, unlike the guys at the Quick Lube, the worst one being Eddie Boone—a short, wild-haired man with a big mouth who still gets a kick out of saying stuff like, "There's another helicopter, Abe, get your laser and see if you can't signal it."

It'd almost be easier if he had nobody to blame but himself, but that's not the case. If a man named Eric Rudolph hadn't built bombs out of PVC pipe and gunpowder, and if this same man hadn't been spotted by an eyewitness who scratched down his license plate as he fled from an abortion clinic where he'd remotely detonated one of these bombs, and if CNN hadn't reported that Rudolph was a suspect before officers reached his trailer, and if Rudolph hadn't seen this on TV and quickly gathered supplies and disappeared into the surrounding mountains before the sheriff's department could arrest him, things would be different. The U. S. government wouldn't have offered a million-dollar reward for his capture, and the FBI wouldn't have busted down the doors of people they'd incorrectly ID'd as having info, wouldn't have interrogated people and trespassed and pissed off the entire town, including Wayne Burchfield, a man who fired a few rounds into the warehouse that functioned as the Feds' HQ, one of his bullets whizzing past an agent studying data on a computer monitor, mere millimeters from the man's skull. The helicopters that'd been used to search for Rudolph from above—heat sensors delivering false readings, thanks to the mountains' heat-retaining rocks—wouldn't have been dispatched to track down the shooter, meaning that one of those helicopters surely wouldn't have hovered a hundred yards from Abe's house, as though waiting for Abe to investigate, which Abe had done. In that case, he wouldn't be standing on his porch right now, afraid of what might happen should he leave. But here he was.

"Fuck it," Abe thinks. He steps off the front stoop into the yard. He's barefoot, but the grass beneath his feet feels slimy, like something other than rain—something warm and viscous—has been falling. He slides out his wallet, removes a business card. MORRIS MASHBURN, PROBATION OFFICER, the card reads.

If Mashburn had taught Abe anything in the last three

months, it was that he could show up at any time. He might
come in the morning, before Abe got out of bed. He might
come in the middle of the day, when Abe was at work, leave
a tube of notebook paper inside one of the empty rings of
Abe's O'Doul's six-pack that said, *Hope this is as strong
as you got.* He might come at supper, tell Abe not to get
up, then slide a biscuit off his plate, sink his teeth into
the buttery middle, wink, and replace it. He might come—
in fact had come—in the middle of the night, Suburban
headlights blazing through the master bedroom window.
He might come for three days straight or skip an entire
week. He might come ten minutes after he'd left. His job,
he said, was to make Abe's life a sort of living hell—to
make him think about what he'd done and that no matter how cute he thought he was being, under no circumstances should he mess with the government, unless he
had a desire to spend the rest of his life in federal prison,
where there were plenty of men about four times his size
who'd love a little mountain man for a girlfriend.

Abe can see Mashburn in his head as he hits the digits
of his cell phone: bald, six-four, with the face of a lion and
the body of a bear.

"Hello?" a voice says.

"Mr. Mashburn?" Abe says.

"None other."

"This is Abe Tucker."

"Laser man!" Mashburn says. "What can I do for you
this evening?"

Abe gives him the rundown, wonders if Mashburn
might make an exception tonight, let him drive around,
see if he can turn up something about his missing
daughter.

"Tell you what," Mashburn says, lips smacking.
It sounds like he's eating meat off a bone. "I'm here at
Robbinsville, paying a visit to this boy who burned down

his daddy's house. I got ten minutes 'fore I head on outta
here. Plus the thirty it'll take me to come on over your
way, assuming I decide to come see you and that I abide
by the speed limit. You do the math."

"So wait," Abe says. "You *are* coming to see me?"

Mashburn crunches some more. "Haven't decided," he
says, "but the longer you sweet-talk me, the likelier I am
to make an appearance."

Abe punches OFF on the cordless. "Let's go," he yells.

"Where?" Tommy yells back.

"To find your sister."

"But you ain't allowed."

"Just talked to Mashburn. We got less than an hour."

Tommy sits up. "But what about my project?"

"What project?"

"The interview."

"What about it?"

"It's due tomorrow."

"Tomorrow? What'd you wait so long for?"

"Dad! I've asked you every night for like a week."

Abe shuts his eyes. The interview was one in a string of
Tommy's endless school projects, this one requiring that
he track down an important person in his community and
ask him a series of questions. Tommy had wanted to interview someone who'd been playing a role in the Rudolph
manhunt. He'd tried to get hold of somebody down at the
FBI HQ, but hadn't gotten past the makeshift guardhouse.
He'd left messages on the deputy police's voice mail, even
tried to interview George Nordmann, the guy who owned
the health food store downtown and whose house Rudolph
had broken into a while back, helping himself to a variety of dried fruit and meat and beans, leaving five crisp
hundred-dollar bills on the kitchen counter. The whole
thing had spooked Nordmann so bad that he set to sleeping on the floor of his store, plastering his windows with

newspaper so the media couldn't see in. In the end, none
of these potential contacts materialized, so Tommy ended
up settling for the next best thing: dear old dad.

"Whatever," Abe says. "Bring your recorder. We'll do
some on the way."

"On the way to where?"

"Your mom's."

Before today, it had been sixteen days since Abe called
Gina, a fact he hopes she's noticed, since it supports the
theory that he's cool with their trial separation thing,
even if Gina's never used the word *trial* to qualify the
word *separation*. He hopes that Gina will interpret his
not-calling as a kind of thoughtfulness, a way of demon-
strating his ability to empathize with how a thirty-eight-
year-old mother might need some space, some time to
recuperate after accidentally screwing a man, twenty
years her senior, a man named Len Hogsed, who manned
for years a deli counter at Ingle's grocery until the manager watched a security tape that revealed Gina and
Len engaging in "relations inappropriate to the work-
place," a phrase that, nearly five months after the fact,
still has the power to transform Abe's chest into a rick-
ety barrel of gunpowder, one whose fuse has just been
lit and whose spark is inching inevitably toward a deto-
nation of massive proportions. But as angry and sick as
the thought of Hogsed makes him, he likes to indulge a
fantasy where Gina comes to her senses, says stuff like,
"Baby, I don't know what happened to me" and "I'm sorry,
I just lost it there for a little while." He'd love the chance
to act self-righteous, to recount the ways her cheating had
wrecked him, but also imagines her burying her face in
his chest and weeping, the crush of her body against his,
the way her crazed remorse would dissolve his anger. Of
course he'd forgive her. He'd even learn to forget. Maybe,

he thinks, that's one of his problems. She can sense his eagerness for absolution, finds it distasteful. If that's the case, then it's finished. Game over. Because he doesn't know how else to be.

Tommy presses a button on the side of the recorder, holds it to his mouth. "Please state your full name," he says. He then tilts the recorder toward Abe, who's trying to back the truck out of the driveway without running into the ditch.

"Shouldn't you skip the ones you already know?"

Tommy sighs, presses stop, rewinds the tape. "Ms. Munsen said to act like we don't know anything about the person, even if we do."

"Fine."

He presses record again. "Please state your full name."

"Abraham Frederick Tucker."

"Okay, Mr. Tucker, can you name some accomplishments that have given you the most satisfaction in life?"

"Accomplishments."

"Stuff you're proud of."

"I know what accomplishments are. I'm thinking."

What he's also doing, now that they are on the road: keeping his eyes peeled for Alex. As they coast past houses and trailers, each one alive with TV light, he scans yards, car hoods, porches. Nobody.

"So?"

"I don't know. I guess it'd have to be raising you and your sister."

"Can you elaborate?"

Abe racks his brain. It seems shameful to not know how to articulate how lucky he is to have relatively smart, healthy kids, how he misses Tommy and Alex when they're at Gina's, even though it's usually a matter of minutes after they return that they start fighting over the remote or PlayStation controller, then it's "Okay guys, time to do

your homework!" then "Get your butts in here for supper!" then "By God, one of you's gonna help me fold this
laundry!" Once it's time for bed, Abe's usually too tired to
reflect on his blessings, though that doesn't stop him from
staying up, since if he goes to bed when his kids do, he'll
feel like he hasn't carved out enough of the day for himself, not to mention that the earlier he retires, the longer
he has to lie there in bed, alone, missing Gina, wondering
what exactly it is that she doesn't like about him and if
she was lying when she said that no, he hadn't done anything in particular to drive her away and that she didn't
find him repulsive, but that she just needed space, needed
time, that she'd never really had either and wanted to
know what it felt like to do whatever she wanted, to not
feel tied down, and that yes, she knew that was selfish but
that was how it was, and she didn't expect him to understand or even respect it, didn't even want him to. She just
wanted him to *leave her alone*. It would've been easier,
he thinks, if she'd just said, "Eat shit and die" or "I hate
you." So he tries not to think about it.

"Next question," Abe says.

Tommy holds the page up to the vanity mirror light.
"What. Is. Your. Greatest. Weakness?"

The truck lurches forward. "Sometimes," Abe says, "I
can be blind. Sometimes I don't see things like I should.
Which leads to questionable decisions."

"Like with the helicopter."

Abe winces. "Do we have to discuss that?"

Tommy presses stop on the recorder. "You said you'd
do this."

"I'm doing it!"

Tommy presses record again. "Then explain what happened on May 11, 1997."

"Fine," Abe says, settling back in his seat, going with
the flow, thankful, actually, that Tommy is here to keep

him distracted. "May 11. Saturday. You and Alex and Mom had gone to Six Flags. I'd come in from mowing to drink a beer and I'd found your old laser pointer in between the couch cushions, so I was using it to shoot whatever I saw on TV. Wasn't getting a whole lot out of it, just nothing else to do.

"Eventually, I heard this helicopter. Didn't think much of it. They'd been running those things day and night looking for Rudolph. Anyway, I was sitting there shooting the TV, waiting on that helicopter to pass but it never did. Sounded like it was sitting on top of the house. Windows rattling like crazy. I stuck my head out the front door and saw it above the pines on the hill behind the house. And I was like, huh, maybe they finally cornered ol' Rudolph. And because we own that hill I figured I had a right to check out what was happening. So I did. But not much was. Trees were swaying, pine needles flying everywhere, but that was it. I finished my beer, put the empty on the ground, stomped it. Then it hit me: What if nobody's in the helicopter? What if it's some new FBI gadget, and somebody back at HQ's running this thing remotely? So for shits and giggles I pointed the laser pointer at the chopper, wondered if it'll reach. Then— and seriously, don't ask me to explain this one, because I can't—I pressed the button."

They've stopped at a red light near the end of Main. In the old A&P parking lot, a boy about Alex's age fails to master a wobbly skateboard.

"Wait a second," Abe yells. "Hey kid!"

The kid's wearing a T-shirt as big as a dress and baggy jeans. He flips his bangs out of his face. He's holding something between his finger and thumb. A cigarette? A joint? Abe can't tell.

"Yeah?" the kid says.

"You know Alex Tucker?"

"I dunno." He casually slips whatever he's holding behind his back.

"She's about your height," Abe says. "Brown hair. Cute."

The kid shrugs.

"Seen anybody that fits that description?"

The kid shakes his head. He's got that look—like somebody with a secret he'll never reveal. Abe wonders if maybe he's the one—the kid from Alex's bus. But there's no way to know.

When Abe imagines it—not because he wants to, but because it happened and he doesn't know how—he imagines that boy putting his hand on her head. The hand on the head—it's the worst part. If it was up to him, and it isn't, since Principal Trueblood refuses to give him a name, he'd hunt that boy down and beat him to a pulp. Okay, maybe not pulp. But he'd at least break a few fingers on the hand he imagined the kid placed on Alex's head, so that for the rest of the little bastard's life, the hand would sing out periodically in an arthritic fugue. Of course, this finger-breaking deal might be costly in terms of lawyer's fees, not to mention that it'd violate Abe's parole, thus landing him back in jail, where they'd put him after the chopper incident. So he's not only failed to find the boy and break his hand, but also he hasn't even mentioned the situation, not to Tommy, Alex, or Gina, instead keeping it stored safely inside his head, where he's been rehearsing a speech, for Alex's benefit, that'll explain why what she did isn't really that bad and that no matter what anyone says she shouldn't feel ashamed, though she should also know that what that boy asked her to do wasn't making love.

Most of Abe's opportunities to deliver this speech seem to occur after he's refilled the O'Doul's can with Bud. For instance, last night, after his fourth beer, he stopped by Alex's room to talk. For the first time, he noticed the walls of her room were bare, walls she'd once plastered with pictures of horses, models, boy bands, and inspirational posters, one of which featured a kitten dangling from a tree and the caption, "Hang in there!" Apparently, she'd tossed everything, including the dream catcher that'd hung for ages in her window, the one she'd bought that time they drove out to Cherokee. They'd gone to Cherokee because every time the kids went to Walmart they passed a billboard with a feathered Indian extending a tomahawk, and they'd been begging Abe and Gina forever to go, so they went, despite Abe's protests that the whole thing was a giant rip-off and a shame to Native American peoples. Once there, they'd observed the caged bears and they'd walked through a re-creation of an Indian village and watched chubby women pound actual corn into actual meal while chubby Mohawked men carved masks from tree bark. Afterward, the kids had wanted to stop for souvenirs. Tommy got a beaded arrow that snapped in two on the way home, while Alex chose the dream catcher, which had struck Abe as odd, since she'd never seemed interested in anything remotely mystical.

However many years later—six? seven?—the absence of the dream catcher seemed like a bad omen, but Abe folded his arms and leaned against the doorframe and said, as casually as he could, "Whatcha reading?" Alex, expressionless, held up a book entitled *Cheat*. The cover showed a blond and a brunette, each dressed in a sweater and skirt and collared blouse, standing in front of a stone wall sheathed in ivy. Alex explained that the book was about a group of boarding school girls enacting revenge upon a popular girl, which caused Abe to wonder, aloud, if that wasn't a little over her head. And instead of answering this question, Alex asked if he'd been drinking. That made Abe frown and say that he'd had a beer with dinner, but he wouldn't call that *drinking*, and she said, "Why bother? With alcohol, I mean," to which he responded "Good question. Get back to me in fifteen years," and then, "But seriously, I want to talk to you."

Alex put down her book and ran a hand through her hair, which was still wet from her bath and probably smelled like those beads she sometimes dropped into the water, but because he wasn't close enough to smell he didn't know. And because Abe no longer had the nerve to ask "Why did you put that boy's thingamabob into your mouth?" he said, "You know your mom and I are try-ing to work things out, right?" And she said, "Yes," and he said, "How do you feel about that?" And she said, "I don't know," and then, out of the blue, no lead-up what-soever, "Sometimes, honestly, I think that you guys just weren't meant to be," an utterance that effectively ended the conversation, though he stood there a few moments more, watching her read, noting for the umpteenth time her catlike eyes and prominent cheekbones—in other words, how she absolutely could not look any more like her mom.

"Dad," Tommy says, "light's green."

The truck lunges forward. The wind's picking up, blow-ing leaves and debris down empty sidewalks. Rain splat-ters the windshield then stops. The effect is as if they'd passed under someone taking a leak.

Lord, Abe thinks, *let her be okay.*

"So," Tommy says, pressing RECORD again, "you pointed the laser at the helicopter."

"Right," Abe says, resuming a posture of reflection—right wrist resting at noon on the steering wheel, left elbow propped against the door. "Well, the next thing I knew, I looked down at my shirt, and there were five red dots hovering over my heart. And I thought, oh my God, this is the way I'm gonna go."

"So what'd you do?"

"Dropped the pointer, yelled, 'I'm unarmed!' I mean, you'd think that with all that equipment they'd be able to tell I wasn't armed. Then ol' Ray Wood drives up in his Bronco. Veers off the road. Drives right over the grass. Kickin' up dirt. Yells at me to get in. So I back away from the chopper, hands in the air, and climb into Ray's truck. Ray says he heard the whole thing over the police scanner: somebody fired a couple of shots into the FBI HQ and they think it was me. 'You've got to turn yourself in,' he says. So he drives me to the station, where, as soon as we pull up, four Suburbans pull up, too, and these guys in all black—"

"Ninja suits?" Tommy asks.

"Yes," Abe says, "the ninja-suited dudes."

Ahead, a faded sign announces *Whispering Meadows*. Abe flips on his turn signal. Trailers blanch as the beams of the truck's headlights swing past.

"Okay," Abe says, "put her on pause."

"Can I go in?"

"Better not," Abe says. He puts the truck in park. Leaves the engine on. "I'm just gonna pop my head inside."

Abe's reflection in the front door's diamond-shaped window tells the story: he looks like a thin-faced, bearded haint. Whatever. He's not here to court. He peeks inside. Gina's in there, sitting Indian-style on a ruptured beanbag, while a television no bigger than a toaster oven blasts a scattershot of light into the room. Gina's studying her forearm, whose smooth white underbelly has been inked in red and blue and green. It's what she does now. Draws on herself with Sharpies. It's a recently discovered talent, one that came as no surprise to Abe, since he'd always admired the cakes she made at Ingle's, cakes that resembled speckled trout or John Deere tractors or a bust with double Ds that looked so sweet and pillowy you wanted to mash your face right between them. Lately, her dream—and she knew this was a long shot, but she believed if she advertised it right, it might work—was to open a salon where people could come and she'd draw on their skin, a place for those who weren't sure about getting a real tattoo. Like, how could you really know if you could live with something permanently until you tried it out temporarily, so why not let an experienced artist try her hand on you first?

Abe turns the door handle and pushes. The door swings open.

"Abe?" Gina says. She's fanning the half-completed boa circling her forearm with a magazine. Her hair's up—a silken helix secured with a pencil—just like he's always liked it, since it reveals the slope of her neck. "You lost your mind?"

"No. Just our daughter."

"What do you mean?"

"She's not at home. Thought she might be here. Is she?"

"No." Gina, now standing beneath the drooping blades of a ceiling fan, is wearing a Tweety Bird T-shirt that hangs mid-thigh, revealing her chunky little legs, which are splotchy with bruises. "Why didn't you call me?"

"I did. Your cell must be dead."

Gina blinks. "Shit," she whispers.

"She didn't say anything to you about having different plans today?"

Gina frowns. "I'm not the one she lives with." Which is true. They haven't worked out a custody agreement because Gina hasn't served him any papers. And Abe's not going to remind her to.

"Well, I'm going to get back in the truck and look."

"I'll do it. You'll get into trouble."

"You don't even have a car."

"I'll get a ride. Did you call J.C.'s?"

"No."

"Well, shit, Abe, that's the first place you oughta look."

J.C. lives on Happy Top, a place that, as it turns out, isn't usually in the best of spirits, unless you mean the alcoholic kind, since it's home to run-down houses and trailers and, in one case, a guy who parks his R.V. on a sun-scorched little plot of piney land and cooks butchered deer meat over a fire pit. J.C., like Alex, is twelve, and dresses funny for someone who claims to be born again, wearing clingy, black-netted shirts and skirts that look like they've been sewn together using strips of pliant metal. She's got rings in her ears and a hoop she slides through her septum after school. Once, Abe found J.C. and Alex in the shed, sharing what looked like a doobie but turned out to be an actual cigar, which, J.C. explained, they were trying only so they could say they'd tried it.

"I don't have J.C.'s number," Abe says.

"It's on my cell. Gimme a second. I gotta find it and plug it in."

"Forget it," Abe says. "Just tell me where she lives."

"Two houses down from Hazel Sharp, in a brick house with yellow shutters."

"Wanna ride with us?"

Gina squints at the truck. Tommy's rolled down his window. He's waving.

"No thanks," she says. She blows Tommy a kiss. "But call me when you find her."

Gina never told Abe why she chose Hogsed or if it was Hogsed who chose her, never relayed a single detail about what happened. Abe knows nothing about how it went down, or if going down had been part of it. Admittedly, it'd kill him to know, but it was killing him not to. He'd tried to argue that that there was room in this failure for him, and was therefore entitled to details, and Gina argued that he just didn't get it, that the details weren't his to know. Fine, Abe had said, he could live with that. But he still thought they needed to stay together, if only for the sake of the kids. He understood a person could go crazy, or temporarily abandon her right mind, but she'd said that wasn't how it was, she'd known exactly what she was doing; that she felt Hogsed, a man with a braid to his waist and an underbite and a big chin and a belly, truly knew her, that for the first time in her life she felt free. Even after Hogsed drove his campered Datsun out of town, never to return, Gina felt that he'd given her something nobody could take away. And whenever Abe tried to figure out what she meant, she'd simply say, "Please" and "Don't" and "Abe, I'm not asking you to wait for me" and "Go on with your life."

As if Abe had any choice: somebody had to take care of the kids.

Nobody talks on the ride to Happy Top. The tape is still going, recording a bunch of nothing, which is exactly what they find at J.C.'s. No lights on. No vehicles in the driveway. Just a lawn blanketed with leaves, a few of which twitch in the wind. *No reason to panic*, Abe thinks, knowing that's what most parents tell themselves in the initial hours after their daughters go missing, knowing there's reason to panic. Why worry, when it's a quarter past nine and he's been gone from the house for forty-five minutes now and has no idea where Alex is, and the two most likely places have turned up zilch, which means she's run away or gotten into a car with an older kid who drove it into a tree, or maybe—worst case scenario—someone had seen her walking home by herself, which she always did, across the playground, then down the hill, and had taken her. But maybe this someone, a teacher, had asked her if she was okay because she'd been crying, which she did sometimes, got teary-eyed for no reason—not for no reason, but because her mother had basically abandoned her, plus who knew how many hormones blazed through a girl's body at this age? And this teacher, who'd been abused as a child and had been keeping whatever sadistic urges in check for as long as he could, had asked her if she needed somebody to talk to and she'd said yes and he'd taken her to his house, which was on the outskirts of town, and they'd gone inside and he'd done what he was burning to do and then it was over, forever.

It turns out that none of these things have happened. It turns out, when they get back to the house, that Alex is there, waiting for them. There, on the floor of the living room, she's eating a Devil's Food Cake bar and watching *Super Nanny*, like nothing's happened. Her hair's in braids. She's wearing all black. Her lips are black. Her face is whitish-gray. She looks like a zombie. Tommy balances himself on the back of the couch, pokes Alex in the cheek, as if testing that she's real. She slaps his hand away.

"Where," Abe says, but his voice breaks. He tries again, at a lower decibel. "Where. The. Hell. Have. You. Been?"

Alex looks up. "Me? What about ya'll?"

"Don't sass," Abe says. "Just answer the question."

Alex rolls her eyes. "I was at church."

"Church?"

"J.C.'s church? Remember? They're putting on the Halloween play? I told you we were practicing tonight."

"What?"

"Dad, don't act dumb. I did. Last night. You were sitting in that chair, watching TV, and I was like, is it okay if I go to play practice at J.C.'s church tomorrow, and you were like whatever."

Last night, Abe thinks. He can't remember.

"Call your mom," he says. "She's worried."

Alex turns up the TV volume. "You call her."

Abe opens his mouth but the speech he'd been revising in his head since five thirty, the one that'd outline the harsh terms of Alex's punishment and possibly shame her into producing an earnest apology, dissolves.

Alex shoves the last bit of cake into her mouth. "What?" she says, still chewing.

"Why do you have to be such a little bitch?" Tommy says.

Without thinking, Abe glances over his shoulder, whips out his hand, and pops Tommy in the mouth with his knuckles. At least, he meant to pop him in the mouth, and not *that* hard, just enough to remind him that he wouldn't put up with that kind of language, especially not directed at his sister, even if she asked for it. But what happens is that the backside of Abe's hand—the one still wearing his wedding ring, even though Gina removed hers—swats Tommy in the nose. The boy's eyes water. He staggers. He goes down on one knee, covers his face with a hand. When he brings his hand away, it's covered in blood.

Tommy stares at the blood, as if unable to comprehend it. He's never liked blood. As a kid, he'd freaked at the sight of it. Just getting the wound to stop bleeding was a task; he didn't want anyone touching it. You had to hold him down. Sit on him.

"Damn," Abe says. "Tommy. Jeez, I didn't mean—"

Tommy gets to his feet. His eyes are glossy with tears.

"Hey," Abe says. "Hey."

Tommy wobbles toward the bathroom, goes in and slams the door. Next: the sound of the toilet paper roll unspooling.

"Nice," Alex says.

Abe points at her. "I did *not* mean to do that."

"He'll get over it," Alex says.

Outside, a car door slams.

Abe pretends not to hear it. He stares at the TV, where a pair of kids are running riotously over furniture. He hears the familiar footsteps approaching and, a few seconds later, the brisk one-two-three-four-five knock that makes the plastic on the screen door shiver. Then the door swings open and Mashburn steps in. A pair of bug-eyed sunglasses rest on his head. His windbreaker's beaded with water. Mud-chunks hug the sides of his boots.

"Greetings," he says.

"Evening," Abe says.

Alex stands, balls up her napkin, walks briskly past Mashburn, giving him a smirk as she passes. She continues down the hall, to her room. She slams the door.

Mashburn stands there, hands on his hips. "Was it something I said?"

Abe shrugs. "I don't know if she appreciates you the way I do."

Mashburn grins. He surveys the room. "Where's the boy?"

"Just turned in," Abe says, hoping Mashburn won't go in there and see Tommy with a wad of balled up toilet tissue pressed against his nose and tears running down his face and ask what the hell happened.

"I brought him something," Mashburn says. He stuffs a hand inside his jacket, rummages around, pulls out a wadded up T-shirt, tosses it to Abe.

Abe catches it, holds it up. The front of the T-shirt features the most recent police sketch of Rudolph's face. He's got his hair pulled back into a ponytail. His face, serene and handsome and not un-Jesus-like, is stubbled with whiskers. Below his face, there's a caption that says, "This is as close as I'm gonna come to $1,000,000!"

"Huh," Abe says.

"Thought he'd like to have it," Mashburn says.

Abe nods.

"Looks like things have calmed down around here."

Abe nods again.

"Guess I'll head out to Hangin' Dog. Got one more destination before I turn in."

"Appreciate you stopping by," Abe says.

"My pleasure," Mashburn says.

Abe does not drink three to four beers after Mashburn leaves. He doesn't watch TV, doesn't make himself a plate of crackers and cheese. He doesn't stand at Tommy's door and demand to be let in, doesn't beg for forgiveness. Doesn't call Gina, doesn't say another word to Alex about calling her. At one point, the phone rings. Nobody answers it. He takes it off the hook.

Abe lies on the couch with the Rudolph T-shirt over his head. He doesn't think about Gina or Hogsed or Tommy or Alex or Mashburn or the kid whose pecker Alex supposedly licked. He pretends that the shirt's a filter through which he can see Rudolph. And then there he is. The fugitive has not, as some have predicted, absconded to Amsterdam. He's still right here in these mountains. He's living on his own terms, at the edge of a rhododendron brake. Not that his terms are all that great. The ground is rock hard beneath his back, and even if he has an inflatable mattress in whatever cave or lean-to he's hunkered down in, he's never one hundred percent comfortable, never gets more than two hour's sleep at a time. And tonight, Abe sees, he's wet. And cold. And miserable. His squirrel traps are empty. He ate his last handful of trail mix the day before, hasn't eaten a thing since. In fact, he doesn't look well. He's just lying there on the ground. Nothing moves except his face, which is grimacing. Maybe he fell, Abe thinks, broke his leg. Or worse, he's paralyzed. Abe zooms in for a closer look. He sees something. Some kind of animal. He can't tell what it is. Perhaps something thought to be long extinct. But one thing's clear. It's ferocious. And hungry. In fact, it's chewing on Rudolph's leg. My God, it's eating him, Abe thinks. Abe can't believe what he's seeing. He lies completely still, trying to comprehend what it must feel like: the teeth of something terrible tearing you up, bit by bit, and you, completely aware, completely awake, can't do anything but watch.

The Visiting Writer

MY PHONE RANG but I couldn't answer; I needed both hands to steer. I was attempting to pass an eighteen-wheeler that had fishtailed twice, its tires swerving onto the highway's ribbed shoulder, producing that awful thrum intended to wake sleeping drivers. It was easy to imagine the truck veering into my lane, nudging me toward the concrete retaining wall. Sparks would fly. I'd be crushed, burned alive, a screeching corpse of hot cinders. The visiting writer—who I was scheduled to pick up at the Star City Airport—would, after compulsively checking her phone or her watch or a clock on the wall, slowly arrive at a realization: somebody, somewhere, had made a mistake.

Whether I wanted to pick up the visiting writer was beside the point: I had volunteered six months before and the day was now here. There was no reason to feel intimidated; I'd picked up a number of visiting writers over the years and found the task to be pleasant and, at times, rewarding. Furthermore, if I remembered to

submit the correct paperwork to a woman in my department (who wore two pairs of glasses at the same time and
draped purple costume jewelry over her cable knit sweat-
ers), I would be reimbursed for my trouble: a deposit of
fifty bucks to my checking account, an amount that far
exceeded the price of the gas I would burn.

More importantly, the return trip to the University
Inn—a forty-minute commute through blue-tinted
mountains—allowed me to acquaint myself with strangers who'd penned critically lauded literary work. A
year before, I'd chauffeured a famously mustachioed
Californian who'd revealed that his most frequently
anthologized story—in which the main character was
shot in the head—had been structured to represent the
geography of a brain: the story's single space-break symbolized both the trajectory of the bullet and the bisec-
tion of the organ's right and left hemisphere. On another
occasion, as a way of attempting conversation with a
flamboyant writer who also happened to be the found-
ing editor of a famous New York literary magazine, I'd
mentioned that I'd once met a woman who'd claimed to
have worked as his personal masseuse, an assertion that
inspired the man to bellow, in an aristocratic brogue,
"Why I've never had a massage in all my life, not even in
a Thai bordello!"

Though most of our visiting writers had exhibited idio-
syncrasies of one variety or another—one elder poet had
unsnapped a leather valise in which his own personal
scotch decanter had been securely strapped; another
writer, who specialized in something she called "experimental hypertext," had requested a two-day supply of
organic carrot juice that was to be delivered to her hotel
room—none of them had ever said anything offensive or
exhibited disturbing behavior. Their words and actions
had never suggested I had anything to fear.

The writer I was now on my way to retrieve, however, was of a different ilk. Despite having been a finalist for the Pulitzer, the National Book Award, the National Critic's Circle Award, and the PEN/Faulkner, it was safe to say that her name wouldn't have rung the average American reader's bell. Yet, among readers of so-called literary fiction, she was well known. Critics had used words like "dark" and "disturbing" and "morbid" to describe her work, which revealed a preoccupation with violence and sexual deviance. Those familiar with the visiting writer's biography would recall that she had worked in her youth as an exotic dancer and prostitute, and might presume that these experiences had informed, to a degree, her fiction. I wish I could say that I had drawn no conclusions based on the facts of the visiting writer's life, as I know quite well that people have good reasons for the seemingly inexplicable things they do, but the truth was that when I thought of the visiting writer or saw her blown-up author photo on the posters tacked to bulletin boards across campus—a portrait of a severe-looking woman whose wide-eyed stare suggested she might be unhinged, even deranged—I envisioned a person who had been nourished by forces I couldn't help but imagine as malevolent.

Upon arriving at the Star City Airport, I struck a casual pose—driving with the underside of my wrist on the top of steering wheel—and drifted slowly along the one-way road encircling the long- and short-term parking lots. Thick-bodied mountains—reduced to jagged blobs, now that the sun had sunk behind ridgelines—rose in the distance. Giant flags flapped in wind. A chunky police cruiser sat before a set of doors that led to TICKETING.

I swiped the screen of my phone, thinking that perhaps my wife had called, I tapped Recent Calls. An unfamiliar number appeared. Because the caller had failed to leave a message—and because I am often at the mercy of my own curiosity—I thumbed the number. Three rings later, a voice greeted me. It was breathy and deep.

"My flight's delayed," she said.

"Oh no," I said.

"I hate to inconvenience you," she said.

"It's fine."

"How's the weather?"

"Clear skies. A little wind."

"No snow?"

"Not even a drift."

"Then we have nothing to fear."

"I suppose not," I replied, and said I'd see her soon.

The visiting writer's flight was delayed twice more. I circled the lots, trying to evade the kind of resentment that brought the very notion of a "visiting writer" into absurd relief. In other parts of the world, humans were abducting and torturing other humans. Melting ice caps were releasing greenhouse gases. Poachers were slaughtering endangered ruminants and harvesting their horns. And here, in Star City, a university representative was wondering when he should park his nondescript minivan—a vehicle he wouldn't have been caught dead driving a decade before—at a ten-minute loading zone, to minimize the distance a visiting writer would need to traverse between modes of transportation. Because it wasn't enough to hand the visiting writer a check for ten thousand dollars—an amount this representative might've used to purchase a new washer and dryer, and to install energy efficient windows, and to replace rotten siding on the southern side of his house—one had to treat her like royalty, had to ensure every whim was met, had to inquire about when and with whom she would take her meals, had to arrange transportation between the University

Inn and wherever she was scheduled to present a talk on the craft of writing, returning her afterwards to the Inn so she could refresh herself before embarking upon the arduous job of reading her work—like a mother delivering a bedtime story to an audience of notebook-toting undergrads. A brief book-signing would ensue, followed by a trip to a faculty member's home, where attendees would clump together over bottles of craft beer and glasses of box wine, holding plates of hors d'oeuvres prepared by an underpaid deli worker, while the less inhibited—and no doubt most obnoxious—guests would corner the visiting writer and, in a predictably nauseating display of ingratiation, pepper her with questions about this or that friend at this or that university until a designated chauffeur intervened and transported the exhausted and half-inebriated writer back to the Inn, where, thanks to an indigestible meatball she'd hoisted—via toothpick—from a bubbling crock pot, she would sleep fitfully until four, when she'd answer the bleat of her ringing phone and, in the moments before she recalled having requested a wake up call so she wouldn't miss that day's only flight to New York, wonder who in the world would have the nerve to phone at this hour.

Then again, what did I know? As an untenured professor, I depended upon a world of illusions to sustain my artistic legitimacy. Aside from the dozens of emails and recommendations and revised major check-sheets and minutes for meetings and annual reports, I hadn't completed a draft of anything in more than a year. I'd spent the better part of a decade thinking of myself as a writer who was "emerging," though what I was emerging from, exactly, it was impossible to say. Once upon a time, I'd published a novel—copies of which were available on eBay for a penny, plus shipping and handling—with a seemingly reputable independent press that, in the wake of the Great Recession, replaced the majority of its staff with interns, all of whom answered to a pathologically elusive editor who, whenever I called, was described by a cheerful receptionist named "Guy" as having just stepped outside for a cigarette, but would, I was promised, return my call as soon as possible. He never did.

Moreover—and perhaps most significantly—I had never been a visiting writer myself. Representatives from other universities and colleges made no inquires concerning my availability. No school had assigned my novel as an upcoming "common book," to be read by an incoming freshmen class. I had not enjoyed an all-expenses paid trip to a city university or idyllic college town, and so had been neither wined nor dined. My work, though it had been described as "iconoclastic" on a blog that promoted so-called "experimental" literature, had earned a grand total of zero awards. I published a story here and there, in obscure journals edited by grad students desperate to fill their pages. My payment for these stories—manuscripts I'd labored over, in many cases, for *years*—would be two contributor's copies of the issue in which my work appeared (alongside authors whose names I didn't recognize, but who also taught at second-tier universities), as well as a form allowing me to purchase "additional copies at a reduced rate," a phrase that never failed to fill me with despair.

I checked my face in the mirror of an airport bathroom. Dark circles orbited my eyes. My forehead resembled clay that had dried and cracked. Flakes of skin peppered my nose. I was in no condition to meet anyone, much less an accomplished visiting writer who might immediately and correctly assume that I was her intellectual inferior. I rubbed my hands with berry-smelling soap. Faucet sensors refused to register my presence. I slung soapsuds onto the floor, ripped a towel from the stingy dispenser.

In the main lobby, arriving passengers descended an escalator: a goateed man in a football jersey; a crop-topped teenager, a hoodied grandmother wearing pajama bottoms. Finally, the visiting writer appeared. Her hair—white, streaked with gray—framed her face like a set of curtains. She wore a white blouse, white slacks, and white cowboy boots. She might've just come from a small-town theater production where she'd played a benevolent, if slightly disoriented, ghost.

I shook the visiting writer's hand, which was soft and cool. I stated my name. The visiting writer said it was nice to meet me. She stared at me with pursed lips, as if awaiting instruction. I asked about her flight; she said it was fine. "But I can't stop thinking about that plane," she said. "You know, the Malaysian one?"

She meant the Boeing 777, whose disappearance had been dominating American media. I didn't say that one of my daughter's friends—a Chinese girl who, thanks to her skills as a black belt in Tai Kwon Do, could chop an apple in half with her bare hand—knew an entire family who'd been onboard. Instead, I asked the visiting writer what she thought. She was, she admitted, no expert. But she suspected the pilots were to blame.

"Every time I board an airplane," I said, "I think to myself, 'This is the end.'"

The visiting writer chuckled.

I smiled, pleased to have made her laugh.

At the baggage carousel, I retrieved a steel-colored suit-case the visiting writer identified as hers. She squatted, unsnapped a lever, and raised the lid; she wanted to make sure she'd packed the manila envelope containing her manuscripts. At first, I stared directly into the case but then realized I was eyeballing the visiting writer's clothes—and likely her intimates. A T-shirt emblazoned with a woman's painted face sparkled with sequins. I averted my gaze.

The visiting writer located a bloated envelope, gave it a few squeezes, then stuffed it back inside. "Think we might be able to grab a bite to eat?" she asked, clicking the case closed.

"There's not much around here," I said, envisioning the chain restaurants that orbited the airport. "But the kitchen at the University Inn might be open."

"Wonderful," she said.

It was late, but the visiting writer needed to be fed. I asked if she was ready to go. Her mouth opened like a gash, revealing every one of her teeth.

"Don't be surprised if you never hear from me again," I'd said to one of my colleagues, who'd wondered if I was apprehensive about chauffeuring this particular visiting writer. "It's possible that she might mate with me," I added, "and then devour my head."

Comparing the visiting writer to a ruthless female insect was not, I'll admit, the kindest of assessments; it wasn't even that great a joke. I didn't really think that the visiting writer—however bleak her insights about the human condition might be—posed any kind of predatory danger. Perhaps the hypothesis about forced copulation and subsequent head loss simply allowed me to safely express my own transgressive fantasy—one that I'd indulged as an adolescent, when the sumptuously-worded erotica of a writer of vampire novels had proved legitimately arousing—in which I was overpowered by an older, phantasmagoric woman. Maybe the part where the visiting writer killed me praying-mantis-style was nothing more than a manifestation of my own guilt for having made the joke—or entertained the thought—in the first place. Maybe—and this is the interpretation I find most convincing—the visiting writer represented the kind of person I fantasized about becoming: someone who, despite having passed through the valley of the shadow of very bad things, had emerged, if not unscathed, then undeniably formidable.

At the front desk of the Inn, the visiting writer slid out a credit card and a driver's license. The attendant entered information into a computer.

"You two together?" he asked.

"No," I said. "I'm just escorting her."

Blood rushed to my face. *No*, I wanted to say, *not that kind of escort*. Instead, I feigned obliviousness. If the word, which seemed to hover in the air above us, had suggested anything sordid, the visiting writer registered no reaction.

She was clearly more interested in where she might find food. The attendant explained that the lounge was open until midnight, the kitchen for another hour. "Wonderful," she said. She thanked me for the ride. Said that, from here on out, she should be fine.

Assuming that the visiting writer would politely decline, but feeling compelled, in my capacity as a university representative whose job it was to ensure his guest had everything she needed, I asked whether she might enjoy some company during dinner.

"Actually," she said. "That'd be nice. Let me put up my things and I'll be right down." She disappeared down a hallway whose carpet was patterned with maroon and orange diamonds; I slid out my phone and texted my wife, who, at this hour, would no doubt be curled up in bed, binge-watching a show that followed the survivors of a zombie apocalypse.

"Don't wait up," I typed. "Writer's requested my presence at dinner."

Within seconds, a speech bubble—with three undulating dots—appeared.

Then, inside it: "Bon appétit."

The lounge was mostly empty. A suited man and a woman wearing a trench coat sat at the bar. Above them, a television blazed with highlights from March Madness. I wondered what this couple might assume about the visiting writer and me, sitting as we were at a candlelit table for two. Might they mistake us for mother and son, or even—despite our obvious age difference—for lovers?

As my tablemate studied her menu—her eyes roving behind stylishly oversized, black-rimmed glasses—I imagined an alternate reality, one in which my wife and child were no longer with me, having perished in a tragic car accident, a scenario which I'd been using for years to torture myself with whenever they were late coming home. In this nightmarish realm, I was a man who, like the visiting writer, had known devastation and loss. Our shared agonies might, over the course of an evening, create around us an invisible membrane, under which the particulars of our suffering could intermix, a cosmic transfusion granting our mutual devastations the kind of energy we'd need once we left the table and went our separate ways, promising to meet again soon, maybe even five minutes after we'd paid the bill, in the darkness of the visiting writer's room, where she would teach me how to appreciate the slender boundary separating pleasure from pain.

The waiter—a young man whose askew bow tie granted him a naïf-like charm—delivered our drinks: a glass of cabernet for the visiting writer, a scotch on the rocks for me. The visiting writer wondered whether the tomato bisque was cream-based. The waiter confirmed that it was. The visiting writer then inquired about the duck confit: Any good? The waiter apologized; he hadn't yet sampled that dish. The visiting writer agreed to try it anyway. Although I wasn't hungry, having already eaten dinner with my family hours before, I ordered an entrée that I hoped might signify rationality and restraint: a spinach salad with tofu.

The visiting writer had no trouble making conversation. Ideas occurred to her and she articulated them. She mentioned that her next reading would be in Kansas City. And Kansas City would, she predicted, be a disaster.

"I have two brothers there," the visiting writer explained. "Both excessively obese."

"Wow," I said.

"Three hundred pounds each," she continued. "Perpetually chock full of pains. Doctors can't figure them out. Could be fibromyalgia. Might have something to do with their diabetes."

"They *both* have diabetes?"

"And swollen feet. Not to mention that the number of painkillers they take would most likely prove fatal for the average person." The visiting writer supposed their afflictions were hereditary. She had no idea why she'd escaped such a fate.

The visiting writer made no inquiries about my family. I didn't brag about my wife, whose work on Decision Theory had been lauded by the likes of the Wharton School of Business, and who had been so keenly desired by our institution that she had bargained for—and subsequently won—a spousal hire. I didn't launch into a description, as I often did when making conversation recently, of my eleven-year-old daughter's recent obsession with a photo-sharing social media app, and that she now spent the majority of her free time taking pictures of herself wearing sunglasses or of the strawberry sandwich

cookie she was about to "crush" or simply posting kis-
sy-face Emojis to a variety of boys' comment streams, and
that such activity—however innocent, however ultimately
naïve—suggested a new and disturbing universe was on
the verge of expanding.

"Care for some duck?" the visiting writer asked.

Though I'd never much liked duck—the word sum-
moned smiling beaks and orange flippers—resisting the
writer's generosity struck me as uncouth.

"Sure," I said. "Assuming you have any to spare."

The visiting writer took her knife and began sawing
through the dish's casing—a crepe enfolded around glistening meat. She was, I realized, carving me a bite. If she
raised the fork to my face, and I ate—my lips touching the
tines she'd been sliding into and out of her mouth—what
might that mean? What kind of signal might I be sending?
Before I could answer, the visiting writer tossed, with little
fanfare, a heap onto my plate. I scooped it up and ate.

"Good?" the visiting writer asked.

"Very," I replied. "Much better, actually, than I expected."

She agreed.

The visiting writer did not ask me what I was working
on. She didn't ask what I wrote. However, she did wonder
if I had any thoughts about another famous writer, one
who'd recently published a novel that unfolded in a series
of text messages between a young man and woman, who,
after meeting online, had begun trading descriptions of
bizarre sexual fantasies, which they'd later perform in
public places. In one instance, the woman, standing on a
busy street corner in the middle of the day and wearing
nothing but a hat, a pair of sunglasses and a trench coat,
was approached from behind by the man, who, after lifting her coattails and unzipping himself, penetrated her,

while the woman, turning pages of a newspaper, feigned utter disinterest.

"Everyone seems to be talking about it," the visiting writer said.

"Probably to the chagrin of what's-her-name," I added.

"The ex-girlfriend?"

"Right."

A woman with the same first name as the woman in the novel had recently threatened to file a suit against the writer, saying that he hadn't adequately disguised her and was "defaming her character" through his grotesquely exaggerated depiction of their relationship. The writer had countered by saying that what he had written was fiction, and that nobody would have believed the actual things she had requested he do to her. Their respective arguments had been leaked via social media and subsequently gone viral.

"It's difficult to know who to believe," the visiting writer said.

"Especially when you get the sense that they seem to enjoy hurting one another," I added.

"Or themselves," she replied. Holding her glass by its stem, she tipped back the last of her wine.

"Care for another?" I asked.

The visiting writer placed a hand upon her breast. "I'd better not," she said. "If I have more than one, things tend to..." She wheeled her hand in the air. "Get out of control."

I signaled the waiter.

The visiting writer hoisted her bag—gilded with buckles—onto the table and began to plow through its contents.

"This is on me," I assured her.

"Oh, no," she said.

"Oh, yes," I replied.

"No," she said. "It's my wallet. Don't tell me. Oh, God."

"Can't find it?"

The visiting writer shook her head. Her lips moved but her mouth emitted no sound. She dug with an increasing and clattering ferocity. Once this strategy proved ineffective, she began removing items and setting them on the table. A lipstick. A matchbook. A pink smart phone. A cylindrical hairbrush. A phone charger. A nail file. A ball point pen. A baggie of peanut M&Ms. A box of Parliament Lights 100's. A pillbox with seven lids, each imprinted with the first letter of each day of the week.

"This is very bad," the visiting writer said, shaking her upside-down purse. Unidentifiable confetti snowed onto the table. She stood, patted her pants pockets. Patted them again. She lifted her coat, wadded it up, shook it out. She appeared to be on the verge of losing her mind.

Just then, I remembered something: I had seen the visiting writer set her wallet—a fat, crimson pouch—on a counter at the front desk. I excused myself to check and found it there, unmolested, leaning against a vase of artificial lilies. If the attendant, who'd concealed himself behind a spread open newspaper, noticed my presence, he said nothing.

"Thank God," the visiting writer said, clutching the wallet to her chest. Was she okay? She said she was, though she now was in dire need of a cigarette. Was there a place she could smoke? I supposed we could find one.

She slid a hand around my arm. "Do you mind?" she said. "Just to steady myself."

A heat-flume ignited inside my chest. "Not at all," I said.

"A nice young man like you doesn't smoke, does he?"

"Only when I have a cigarette."

Outside, she flipped the box top, extracted a desiccated-looking Parliament, but couldn't get her match to cooperate. She handed me the matchbook and cigarette. "Maybe you'll have better luck," she said.

I turned my back to the wind. Struck a match. Inhaled. An ember brightened.

"Thank you," she said, after I handed it back. She took an exultant drag. I expected that we might, like a couple of teenagers, share the indulgence. We didn't.

"That," she said, "was genuinely frightening."

"I could tell."

"Sorry you had to witness it."

"I would've reacted the same way," I said. "Losing a wallet, it's like, I don't know. Losing your identity."

"You have experience in that regard?" She tapped the cigarette. Ash scattered.

"I lose my wallet all the time."

"No," she said, "I mean your identity."

I cocked my head.

"It's happening to a friend of mine,'" the visiting writer said, gazing wistfully into the distance. "She loses everything. Enters rooms and can't remember why. She called to wish me happy birthday, then called ten minutes later to tell me again. Anyway, she scheduled a brain scan. And they found a spot."

I grimaced sympathetically. "A spot?"

"More like a dot," she clarified. "They think she had a mini-stroke. Apparently you can have one and not even know."

"That's scary."

"Terrifying," she said. "She's my exact age."

"But you're in good health."

"Ha," she said, waggling the cigarette.

"Everything in moderation," I said.

"Everything?" She raised an eyebrow. Her eyes met mine.

"Most things," I said.

"Ashtray?" the visiting writer said.

"Here." I ground the butt against the sole of my shoe, flicked it behind a shrub.

"You're probably ready to call it a night," the visiting writer said, folding her arms against the cold. She rubbed her shoulders.

I glanced at my watch. Though no numbers registered, I knew that my wife and daughter were sound asleep, and that I'd have to be careful entering the house, slowly twisting the key so the aged deadbolt on our front door wouldn't pop like a firecracker.

"I've got time," I said.

"Good," the visiting writer replied. "Because I just need one more favor. Then I'll let you go." She slid her hand into the crook of my arm, tottered forward and tugged. She seemed simultaneously fragile and strong. Her bones, I imagined, were not unlike those that allowed certain birds to soar and glide: hollow, but durable.

As we passed through the lobby, the attendant nodded, as if granting us his approval. I wanted to explain, but settled for thought-beaming him a sentence: *She just needs one more thing.* He smiled, picked up a phone, and muttered something inaudible.

The visiting writer clung to my arm. My pulse beat against her fingers. Her shoes clacked purposefully against the floor. Elevator doors parted. We boarded. She pressed a button. The numeral five lit up. We began to rise.

"Any idea what you'll read tomorrow?" I asked, remembering the envelope in her suitcase. Its plumpness had suggested a wealth of material.

"I haven't decided," she replied. The elevator was apparently the world's slowest. A ding sounded. The digital readout displayed the number two. "Will the audience be very conservative?"

"It depends on your definition of conservative."

"Let me put it another way." Another ding. Floor three. "Do you think it'd be okay if I read something with some sexuality in it?"

Sexuality, I thought. The word struck me as oddly formal—and, because she had uttered it in such close quarters—erotically charged.

"We're all adults," I said, shrugging.

Ding. Four.

"You know," the visiting writer said. "I recently I read a story of a sexual nature to an audience I expected might be sympathetic. Afterward, a little man, quite indignant, demanded that I explain how I came up with such filth."

"What'd you say?"

"That the supposed *filth* wasn't something I came up with. That it was already there in the world. Had been for ages. Since the very dawn of humanity."

The doors opened. The visiting writer slipped her arm from mine and began walking down the hall. I followed. I'd like to say that I refused to glance at the globes of her glutes or that I hadn't attempted to determine, in the way she walked, whether she was engaging in a sort of sashay. I'd like to say I failed to recall an interview in which the visiting writer had described the novel *Lolita* as something she'd "beaten off to" as an adolescent, or that she'd admitted there was something supremely arousing in having one's limits "totally obliterated" and that though such an event could be frightening, fear had its own particular and undeniable exhilarations. And I suppose I could say all these things. But they wouldn't be true.

The visiting writer slid a card the size of a driver's license into—and out of—a slot.

A light on the locking device turned green.

I followed her inside.

The visiting writer asked me to wait a moment. I wasn't sure I had a choice. Watching her dig through her suit-case, I felt myself teetering on the brink of some preor-dained transgression, one composed by whatever Author was writing the script of my life, in which I was doomed, whether I wanted to or not, to make a tragic mistake. I had imagined, and thus it could be said, *wished for* an escape from normalcy, from the safety of my family—for whom, in a heartbeat, I would have given my life—and from the drudgery of my job, which was the exact job I'd always wanted, and which thousands of other peo-ple, many of them more qualified than I, were striving unceasingly to obtain. As idiotically self-destructive as it was, I couldn't help wonder what it might be like to open up a hole in my life, to slip into a darker realm where I would be utterly—and no doubt deleteriously—transformed.

No, I told myself. I had to remain steadfast. I would, drawing upon reserves of faithfulness, stifle whatever fleeting curiosities might otherwise propel me forward. I would refuse advances. I would cover my eyes if the visit-ing writer began to disrobe. I would turn my head if she beat off to Nabokov. I would, if invited to participate in any indiscretion, politely decline.

But first—because part of me had become noticeably engorged—I needed to rearrange myself. I slid a hand into a pocket to make the shift, but stopped myself. Why conceal something over which I had no control? The vis-iting writer had brought me to her room; this was the result. Why be ashamed? Why not unabashedly inhabit this moment? Wouldn't the visiting writer do the same, supposing she found herself in my shoes?

The visiting writer turned to face me. Her glance fell to my crotch. She tilted her head, as if considering a question, and I thought, this is it: the moment when everything changes. I pushed out my bottom lip, lifted a shoulder, as if to say, *Your move.* It was then that I noticed she was holding a manila envelope, the one containing her manuscripts. The sight of that brown paper—the exact shade of the flimsy envelopes used by the university for Inter-Office Mail—proved disorienting. Did she intend to read me a story? Or might she employ this packet in some kind of game? *You've been a bad boy,* I imagined her saying. And then the envelope—stuffed to the gills with her words—would strike my backside.

The visiting writer's eyes—crystalline blue, incandescent—met my own. I throbbed with anticipation. Was one side of her mouth twisting slyly upward, as if everything was going as planned? She bent the fasteners on the envelope, lifted the flap, and tugged out a page. Then, in the awkward motion that results from a single sheet gathering air as it's transferred from one party to another, she handed me the paper. I blinked at it hard, hoping it might provide further instruction. I read the words printed at the top of the page. I read them again. This was not a set of directions. Nor was it a work of art. It was—and there's no other way to put this—an employment eligibility verification form.

A W-9.

I felt myself deflating.

The visiting writer began to speak in a slightly quavering voice, gradually gaining control. "I would appreciate it," she said, "if you could make sure that form reaches the appropriate parties as soon as possible." She recognized the importance of submitting the requisite paperwork, she said, especially if she ever wished to receive an honorarium. In the case of one recent visit—to a traditionally conservative institution, which, the visiting writer supposed, was enacting revenge for having endured the lewd particulars of the story she had read—she'd been paid not a dime.

I nodded. Rolled the paper into a tube. Knocked it numbly against my leg.

"I probably should get going," I said.

"Yes," she answered. She stared at me hard, then looked away. She seemed like she wanted to say something. Instead, she walked briskly to the door and opened it.

"Have a good night," I said, as I stepped past her and out.

She looked at me briefly once more, from the entryway, her brow furrowed. Then the door clicked shut, followed by the rasp of a chain locking securely—and decisively— into place.

As I descended from the fifth floor to the first, I steadied myself on a handrail bolted to the elevator's mirrored wall. My legs shook. I dared not view my reflection. Behind my closed eyes, the visiting writer's face appeared, the troubled frown that suggested that she was ridding herself of an unwelcome guest. A sickening hollow bloomed within me.

In the lobby, the attendant wished me a good night. Doors parted and I walked outside. Chilled air enveloped me. Bright green leaves—spotlit by floodlights—fluttered in wind. Stars glinted above the stand of pines enclosing the parking lot. I un-tucked my shirt; the tails flapped. On the Inn's fifth floor, a single window was lit. Was it hers? I hoped for some sign of her presence. No woman's silhouette, no trembling apparition appeared.

In the parking lot, I squinted. The minivan was nowhere in sight. I aimed my key in one direction then another, depressing the unlock button each time. No taillights glowed. No horn beeped. I turned to the Inn, to re-orient myself. The once-lit window had gone dark. I raised the key above my head and mashed the button, pressing it again and again, moving deeper into the lot, well past where I knew I had parked. I pledged not to panic. Any minute now, a horn would bleat. An interior light would brighten. Soon, I would be safe in my home. It was, I assured myself, only a matter of time.

Dog Lover

-+>-<+-

JESSIE HAD NEVER called a radio talk show before, had rarely even listened to them—the hosts always sounded so phony and pompous—but today after work she'd gotten into her car, pressed the wrong radio button, and landed on an AM station where a guy named Dale Avortino announced he'd recently seen a study reporting that a significant number of Americans, when asked to rank their closest confidantes, listed their pet as number one. Dale Avortino paused to let this information sink in, then reminded his listeners that he wasn't a scientist or an historian or an anthropologist and that he was only thinking out loud here, but he was willing to bet that if this same study had been done fifty years ago the number wouldn't be nearly as high, and therefore it could be said that this whole my-pet-is-my-best-friend mentality might be an indicator of where we were as a culture slash society. Then he invited those who wanted to share thoughts on this topic to call in.

Jessie rarely used her cell phone while driving (she'd once taken an online quiz entitled HOW OLD ARE YOU...

REALLY? and one of the questions, along with "Are you a smoker?" and "Do you drink?" and "Do you wear a seat-belt?" was "Do you ever use a cell phone while driving?" and if you answered, "yes" that factored negatively into your final score), but today she felt an exception was in order and supposed that this Avortino might be onto something: that maybe we'd evolved to a point where we saw animals as our equals, as opposed to previous times, when humans ate anything that moved and stripped off their skins to use for protection against sun and cold and made instruments from their bones, etc. Of course, way too many animals still suffered unimaginable hardships and torture on a daily basis, but a greater number of people were learning to appreciate them as fellow creatures, to admire and love them as dearly as one would one's own children and were thus more willing to admit that a pet could be one's primary, unequalled best friend. So, with one hand on the wheel, she thrust the other into her purse, found the cell, flipped it open, and tapped out the number with her thumb. On the other end, it rang and rang and rang. Suddenly, a woman said, "Dale Avortino Show, what's your question or comment?" and it took Jessie a second to think, because she had given up on anyone answering; she'd figured the experience would be like calling Ticketmaster on the day that U2 tickets went on sale: you could call until your battery died, but forget about it, you weren't getting through.

"Turn your radio down," the woman said, after she okayed Jessie's comment, then she transferred her to Avortino, who said, "So Jessie from Virginia, you're on."

"Hi, Dale," Jessie said, and, "thanks for taking my call," which she wouldn't have normally said but the woman had coached her to.

"No problem," Avortino said. "So how do you feel about this issue? Is your pet your first and foremost best friend?"

"Absolutely," Jessie said. "I've got a seven-year-old yellow lab named Toby, and he's definitely my very best friend."

"What's so special about Toby?" Avortino asked.

"Well," Jessie said, "we do everything together. We go running and we go for walks, we eat together. He even sleeps between my husband and me in bed."

"Do you talk to Toby?"

"Absolutely."

"And do you think he understands you?"

"I'd say he gets most of what I'm saying."

"Jessie," Avortino said, "who do you enjoy spending time with more, your husband or your dog?"

And Jessie said, "Probably my dog, but that's because we have more in common."

And Avortino said—in a voice that suggested, *Am I hearing you right?*—"You have more in common with your *dog?*"

"I'm a big outdoors person," she said, "and my husband, he's more of an indoors guy."

"Okay," Avortino said, "but don't you think it's a little strange for you to be spending so much time with a dog, instead of with the man you married?"

"Not really," she replied, now unsure as to whether Avortino was just playing devil's advocate, and would come around to a larger point, or if he was setting her up as someone to disdain. "I mean, Toby's not going to be around that long," she said. "His life span's so short, compared to a human's, which means we don't have a lot of time on this earth together."

"Okay, Jessie," Avortino said. "Thanks for your point of view. Appreciate the call."

Jessie closed her cell, turned the radio back up, then punched it off. She felt the spark of adrenaline that accompanied having had her voice broadcast over the radio, but she also felt a little ashamed, because obviously she'd been mistaken—she and Avortino weren't on the same page. Clearly, Avortino didn't have a close connection to an animal, hadn't experienced that particular bond, hadn't known it wasn't something she just dreamed up, which she now wished she would've said during the call: *It's not something I just dreamed up; our relationship, if that's what you want to call it, is real.* Of course, it could've been worse. Could've been more embarrassing. He could've asked something more personal, like how often do you have sex with your husband? Not that she was ashamed about how often they had sex. They had the normal amount, for their personality types. There were plenty of people who didn't have sex much, who didn't need to, and who got by with very little of that kind of thing.

She knew before she opened the apartment door that Toby would be excited to see her and he was, and she was glad: the unselfconscious Toby wasn't ashamed to be predictable. He wagged his tail. He barked when she asked him who her baby was. He jumped on her, and today she didn't say "Toby, down," but sort of danced with him, holding his paws while he licked her hands. She could see it in his eyes: it meant everything to him that she'd come back. He'd been waiting the whole day for this moment, sequestered in the apartment, sleeping, trotting from room to room, sniffing random stuff, maybe tossing Mr. Hanky in the air a few times, lapping some water, who knows, she had no idea what he did all day without her, which made her think maybe what she needed was a web cam, so she could keeps tabs on him from work.

She sat down on the couch. Toby rested his head on her knee, whapped his tail on the coffee table, made some magazine pages splash around. Jessie knew what he wanted: he wanted to go outside, wanted to trot alongside her while she jogged, which she did every day once she got home, logging 3.2 miles on the asphalt greenway that snaked through the neighborhood, letting the Tobester off-leash a few times to chase a squirrel or to do his business. But first she wanted to watch him for a few minutes, to observe and thus appreciate his pre-jog yearning. Toby looked away for a moment, as if he understood what she was doing, and was a little ashamed. His gaze met hers again and his brow raised, as if asking a question: *Can we go now?* Jessie had to purse her lips to keep from smiling.

Without warning, Toby lifted his head, stuck his nose directly into her crotch, basically rammed his face in there, rooted around for a sec, which made her jump back a little, and say, "Tobes, what are you doing?" To which Tobes responded by looking up at her and smiling, at least it looked like he was smiling, though whenever she told her husband, "Look, he's doing it again," Adam would say he didn't think you could call what Toby was doing "smiling," since basically every retriever he'd ever seen looked exactly like that when panting. Jessie had disagreed. What did Adam know about dogs and their capacity for self-expression? How could he look at Toby's face—as she was now—and *not* believe he was observing unabashed doggy joy?

"You are smiling, aren't you?" Jessie said, digging her fingers into his thick neck fur. "Wanna go for a run?" she asked. And because he was a smart dog, who understood absolutely everything he needed to understand, he scrambled to the door, nails clattering against the floor.

Outside, the air was crisp. The sun shone hotly. Green leaves fluttered in the breeze, exposed their pale underbellies. Jessie paused on the stoop, lifted a leg, and rearranged the tongue of her shoe. Toby licked her kneecap. She shooed him away. Then they were off.

Maybe it was how Toby had just unexpectedly rammed his face into her crotch, or the thought of her upcoming

birthday, upon which she would turn the big three-o, or
the fact that she'd been considering how some people not
only really loved but actually understood animals and
allowed themselves to get close to them, sometimes even
too close (like the guy in that documentary Adam had
rented a few weeks ago, about a man who'd died trying
to have sex with a horse, or, rather, died trying to get the
horse to have sex with him, which ugh, she could've lived
without *that* image getting into her brain), but at any rate,
as Jessie walked Toby down a flight of wooden stairs, and
then onto the trail that led to the little neighborhood pond,
which rippled in the distance like molten plastic, she was
reminded of a story—what seemed like an old story or an
urban legend—that she'd overheard a guy from work tell
a group in the break room, about a woman whose friends
decided to throw her a surprise party, and how someone
had to snag the birthday girl's key ring and make a copy
of her house key and return the key ring with the original
to her purse, so that on her birthday, the person with the
key could go to her house while she was at work and let
the party guests in, which he or she did, and how at some
predetermined time the guests streamed in and congre-
gated in the kitchen with the lights off, probably giddy,
because that's how things get in a crowded, dark kitchen
when you're waiting to surprise someone, some people
wondering hey, is this really the best place, what if she
doesn't come into the kitchen, and other people saying of
course it's the best place, everyone always goes into the
kitchen first, but then, *shhh*, they heard the key turning, and her dog, who'd been in the kitchen with the rest
of the people, darted out, and the door opened and she
greeted the dog but didn't return. Nobody knew where
she'd gone. Somebody peeked into the living room but she
wasn't there, it was like she'd disappeared, so a couple of
people started tiptoeing around, and from someplace near

the back of the apartment they heard what sounded like moaning, so they investigated, and there she was, in the bedroom, with her dog and a jar of peanut butter which she must have been keeping there, some of which she'd slathered onto her cootch, and the dog was licking it off, and she was getting off, at least until she noticed who was looking in, then she screamed.

"Ha!" Jessie said, stopping at the grassy incline that led to the back side of a strip mall, where Toby always did his business. Toby cocked his head, as if waiting for a command. Jessie took his face in her hands. "What would you do, Tobes," she said, "if a bunch of strangers barged into our house? Wouldn't you bark? Wouldn't you bite? Wouldn't you show those big old strangers who's boss?"

Toby wagged his tail, licked her palms and forearms. Jessie understood. He was saying, *Your salty arms taste good* and *I love you.*

"Okay," Jessie said. "Go on. Do your business." She unhooked the leash from his collar and watched as he trotted up the hill a ways, sniffed, squatted, and lifted his tail.

"Good dog," Jessie said, thinking how helpless he looked whenever he took a dump. He glanced back at her a couple of times, as if to say, *Seriously? Can you at least like turn your head or something?* Which made her revise her previous hypothesis: how, if a group of strangers did happen to enter the apartment, the dog would not bark ferociously or show anybody that he was boss, unless licking them all to death somehow achieved that partic- ular effect, which she highly doubted. Poor ol' Tobester! So excited about everyone who visited, so always want- ing to play and jump and greet and greet again! This tendency, she knew, was common in dogs, especially of Toby's breed, and it even had a name: "excessive greet- ing disorder." She'd read about it on the Internet, how if your dog happened to be an excessive greeter, you were to ignore him, make zero eye contact, let him know you needed space.

But the sad truth was Toby wouldn't hurt a flea. Unless, of course, the flea happened to be hurting Jessie, then, she expected, and hoped, some sort of primal attack mode would snap on and Toby would go ape shit bananas. It wouldn't matter if the flea in question was a freaking grizzly bear, Tobes would lay into that beast like a devil-possessed wolfhound, which, she figured, was way more than Adam would do, since she was about ninety-five percent sure he'd lie down and play dead.

Back at the apartment, Jessie filled a glass of water, drank half, poured the rest into Toby's bowl. She opened the cupboard, scanned the granola bars and crackers and cans of diced tomatoes, spotted the peanut butter, couldn't help but laugh. Ha! She grabbed the jar, a plastic one that gave a little when she squeezed, unscrewed the top. She put her finger in, scooped out a hunk, offered it to Toby, who lapped it up. "You like that?" Toby tilted his head. "Hmm? You like it?" He wagged his tail. That head-tilt, she thought, so cute and pitiful. It was like, *Come again?* Like, *If you ask me once more, I may actually speak.*

She glanced at the clock. Ten minutes to six. Half an hour from now, Adam would walk in, wonder what they'd have for dinner, suggest they eat out. Once again, the peanut butter jar made itself known. Okay, she thought, no way was she trying that, not even as a joke. It was a stupid idea, maybe even dangerous, though she couldn't imagine why. She pulled off her shorts and underwear, had to before she got into the shower, wondered what did she have to lose, trying it once, just for kicks? Ha! Trying it once? For kicks? Didn't people use similar phrases before they sampled dangerous and addictive substances like crack or meth or heroin, thinking to themselves how much damage could one hit or toke possibly do?—the answer being: A lot. Okay, so you couldn't compare dog tongues to hard drugs, but you had to admit that dog tongues, which often licked shameful areas of their doggie selves and often sampled the dung of other, lesser beasts, might possibly transfer some really hideous bacteria, thus encouraging inflammation or discoloration or hives or who knows what, an idea she immediately rejected as outlandish, having heard, like most people, that a dog's mouth was a hundred—or was it a thousand?—times cleaner than a human's, a fact that had always made sense to her, even if she couldn't explain why: something about enzymes, maybe? Plus, it wasn't like she'd make a *habit* out of this. She was merely performing a personal and private and totally safe experiment, the details of which nobody would know anything about, except herself and Toby, at least until his dog brain completely forgot it ever happened, which, who knew, it might never do, might always wonder, from here on out, whenever the peanut butter came out, whether it was gonna be cootchie pop-licking time, a phase that made Jessie laugh out loud, and so she repeated it aloud: "Cootchie pop-licking time." Ha.

Wearing her T-shirt and socks and shoes but no underwear or shorts, she lifted her foot up and rested it on the kitchen sink for balance, jammed a butter knife into the jar and tried unsuccessfully to spread it on herself. After two failed swipes, the glob plopped to the floor and Toby lapped it up. Already, that was two helpings of peanut butter for the Tobester. How much could he eat before she poisoned him, or at least gave him a tummy ache? She scooped a third glob with the butter knife but this time slid it off with her finger and spread it on herself, thinking this is totally insane, but actually pretty exciting and maybe even fun. One thing, for sure, she hadn't done anything to get her heart rate up like this in a while, years

maybe. She called for the dog to come, Come on, right
here, but again Toby gave her the head tilt, like, *Hey, I'm
already here, what the F do you want?* Okay, she thought,
new strategy. Get on floor, spread legs. Wow. So this position felt a little too vulnerable, like what if when he licked
he got excited and took a chunk out of her, though knowing Toby, he'd never do that, he'd always been very careful when taking food from her hands, seemed to have an
innate sense of restraint.

"Toby," she said again, "come." He came. She patted
herself where the peanut butter was, but he wasn't getting it. She reached for the jar, scooped out another helping, waved it in front of his nose, then guided him down,
but he wouldn't follow. Finally, she got on her back, told
him to stay, then scooted up and toward him, raising
her hips, saying, "Go ahead, lick." Toby hunched down.
Backed up submissively, not understanding. Not getting
the point.

Then, when all seemed lost, he sniffed. Finally, out
came the tongue, and he licked. She shut her eyes, grimaced. Oh gosh. She wasn't sure what to make of that!
Definitely weird, not necessarily great, but not horrible either, a kind of sandpapery swipe that tickled, then
ceased altogether, since after a few licks the peanut butter was gone. Then it hit her and it seemed so dumb.
What she'd wanted was for Toby to understand, to realize it wasn't about peanut butter, but about pleasing her,
about doing something her husband had never done, not
once, not even mentioned, which wouldn't be that big of a
deal if they were close, but they weren't, and might never
be, at least not like she and Toby, who, she'd hoped might
be into it, might in some part of his dog-brain realize that
she liked what he was doing, and because of that he'd keep
doing it. But that's not how it had gone down, which was
okay, maybe even preferable, since who wanted to be the

kind of person who employed her dog in such a service? She sat up, gave Toby a hug, and said, "Would you like Mama to brush you," and Toby's tail whapped against the ground, which meant yes. Then the door opened. Adam was home.

Adam, looking rumpled in his T-shirt and cargo shorts and flip-flops and skuzzy whiskers, carried a leather briefcase. He'd tucked a stack of mail under his arm, held a copy of *Entertainment* magazine in his hand, which he'd already begun to read, already engrossed, probably, in the buzz of an upcoming summer blockbuster. Without glancing up, without seeing his half-naked wife sitting Indian-style on the kitchen floor, the jar of peanut butter within arm's length, brushing the dog with her fingers, he headed straight for the living room, and sat down without a word.

"Hey," she yelled, in a quasi-sing-song way that turned the word into two syllables. "That you?"

"Yeah," he said.

"You're home early."

"Yeah."

"How was your day?"

"Good. Yours?"

"Fine," she said, rising onto her knees, then standing. She scooped up her shorts and underwear, patted her leg, and Toby followed her down the hall. "I'm getting in the shower," she yelled.

"Mm," she thought she heard Adam mumble, though she couldn't be absolutely sure he'd made any sound. She knew he cared about her, knew that him taking her for granted was not only okay but also exactly what he needed out of their relationship, might even also be what she needed, though she couldn't help thinking it'd be nice if, once in a while, he was hungry for her, or that some-day, she would wake up in the middle of the night and he

would be going to town "down there," which was how he
referred to it, as in he would not "go down there," a prefer-
ence which had never been that big of a deal, only because
she hadn't seen much of a reason to make it into a big
deal, and because they could do other things, even if they
usually did only one thing, but still, it struck her as a stupid thing to say, "down there," especially in the tone that
he said it, like "down there" was a food you couldn't bring
yourself to eat, when really, it was much more than that,
was, in some cultures, revered, which made sense, seeing as how everyone, including Adam, had come from his
own mother's "down there," and he should therefore, at
the very least, feel compelled to pay some sort of homage.

"Toby," she said, grabbing Toby's head and looking him
in the eye. "Listen to Mommy. Go to Daddy. Go to Daddy
and give him a big kiss."

Toby cocked his head. He raised his ears and smiled,
tongue lolling. "Go ahead," she said. "Go give Daddy a big
kiss." Toby went.

She peeked out the door to make sure he was going
and he was, trotting down the hall and around the corner.
She smiled. The dog didn't understand everything but he
understood some things, a lot of things, actually, and this
made her happy. She turned the water on, let it warm up,
stepped into the shower and imagined Toby jumping onto
the couch, her husband patting him on the head or, more
likely, snapping his fingers and demanding the dog get
down, since the couch was expensive and Adam wasn't
crazy about dog hair, but then Toby would lean over and
reach out his tongue and lick him, hopefully on his face,
his cheek maybe, or even better, his lips, and Adam would
yell, as he usually did: "Don't lick!" Which, to Jessie,
always sounded completely preposterous, since what was
the point of having a pet if you refused its affections? It
was like having a child and making a rule that he or she

wasn't allowed to kiss you. She could see it now, her husband wiping his face with his shoulder, saying ugh, then
the smell of peanut butter hitting him, and him thinking,
What a waste, giving peanut butter to a dog, Jessie has
got to stop doing that! though surely he would also know
that she never would, that as long as the dog was alive
there'd be no stopping her, she would always spoil the hell
out of Toby.

Scoring

->-<-

MARTIN POSTACHIAN—hailed as Stash by those who know him best—is halfway to Shoe Town when a young woman in a green apron approaches him. "Martin?" she says. "Martin Postachian?" He frowns, trying to place her face. Her brown hair's braided into a single rope. A silver cross rests at the base of her throat. A beatific smile reveals an adorable overbite.

He has no idea who she is. He blames his brain; it's fried.

Normally, after eight hours of reading essays, Stash returns to the bar at the Adam's Mark—a two-and-a-half star hotel overlooking Daytona Beach—and hits the gin with the boys, then the beach, but this afternoon he took a cab—a van, actually—to the mall. He hates the mall, would probably give it a dash, if he had to rate it, since a dash, in the world of Advanced Placement scores, is reserved for something that's so awful, so superfluous that its existence doesn't make sense. But today he needs to buy running shoes. Not that he runs. But he wants to. Mike and Matt and Dave and Ty—four of the two-thousand-plus teachers who convene every year to score the country's A.P. essays—all run. The past two mornings, these guys have risen at sunrise, donned iPods and nylon shorts, and jogged. Meanwhile, Stash, who packed brogues and boat shoes and a pair of Birkenstocks but nothing resembling athletic wear, had slept. When he'd heard the guys were running, he said he'd go, said he'd run barefoot, had heard running barefoot was superior, especially on beach sand, but then it was crunch time, the clock radio bleating ruthlessly, and instead of throwing back his covers, he'd punched "Snooze." When he opened his eyes, Matt stood before him—a wet swimsuit clinging to his ripped legs—saying, Rise and shine numnuts, you missed it, we ran and swam and stabbed a dead jellyfish with a stick of driftwood, plus you know that super-hot Table Leader Moira? The MILF with the five-star rack? She was jogging, too, in a friggin' bikini.

Now, Stash stares at the young woman in the green apron. She's still smiling like she knows him.

"Do I know you?" he asks.

"Sorry," she says, nodding at his chest. "I cheated."

Stash initially assumes she's admiring his blazer, or maybe the equestrian knights on his Burberry tie, or even the classic-fitting Duke waistcoat, all of which his wife, Dana, who has a knack for sniffing out bargains, had snagged from T. J. Maxx clearance racks—an ensemble that, at ritzier chains, might've cost half a grand, but which she walked away with for less than a hundred bucks. Turns out, though, the girl's not admiring his duds. She's eyeballing his nametag, which, he's mortified to realize, he forgot to remove. Sheathed inside a transparent, zippered pocket, it dangles from a shoestringy necklace.

"Inge," the girl says, extending her hand. He squeezes it. She yanks him closer. "So," she whispers, "what do you know about the Dead Sea?"

"The Dead Sea?"

"It lies twelve hundred feet below sea level. Over millions of years, the hot dry air, as well as the evaporation rate, have contributed to an *extremely* high salt content. Thus, it is one of the saltiest lakes in the *world*. In fact, it's so salty, you can float there without trying, even someone like you, who has hardly any fat on his entire body!"

"Well," Stash says, patting his potbelly, "I wouldn't exactly call myself—"

"Wait," Inge says. From a drawer in the kiosk, she chooses a three-toned rectangular block—blue, gray, and white—the size of a new stick of sidewalk chalk. "You're probably asking yourself, why am I telling you about the Dead Sea?" Grabbing Stash's right hand, she rubs his thumbnail. "See those ridges? We're going to totally annihilate those. Then, we're going to restore your nail's natural shine. All thanks to the Dead Sea."

"You don't waste any time, do you?" Stash says.

Inge grins.

Martin Ernest Postachian is a faithful man, as faithful as any man can be expected to be, which is not to say that he never looks at other women, or that he doesn't, on occasion, undress them in his mind, or sleep with them in his dreams, though when this happens, the dreams are almost always nightmares, which he promptly relays to his wife. That's the great thing about Dana: she understands Stash is a highly visual creature, and so, when watching *Entertainment Tonight* or flipping through *Us* magazine, she'll poll him: "Is the woman in question actually hot?" Stash might say, "Uh, yeah?" or "Kind of" or "Nah." Sometimes, she'll even ask for a number, and he'll give her one: 10, 7, 4, 9, whatever. Dana might nod and, like an anthropologist noting the behavior of a peculiar tribesman, emit a non-judgmental "Huh." Dana is not one to be threatened by another woman's beauty. Who else but she could possibly love Martin, who else could tolerate his fascist objection to clutter or his compulsive oven cleaning?

"See?" Inge says. Stash's thumb gleams, as though slathered in polish.

"Wow," he says.

"And guess what? Today, I can give you two kits for fifty dollars. That includes the lotion, the buffer, an extra file, and a cuticle nipper."

Stash winces.

"Come on. Every woman loves manicures. Surely you know a woman?"

There's something endearingly naïve about a girl who believes all women love manicures, or that men—especially one who's lived on Earth as long as Stash—could be persuaded to think so. The truth is, some women would much rather manage the upkeep of their nails without tools. Some women—Dana, for instance—simply employ their teeth.

Plus, as much as Stash would enjoy forking over fifty smacks, if only to reward Inge for an entertaining sales pitch, he can't afford it. The whole reason Dana okayed his attendance at this year's A.P. reading was the promise of that fourteen-hundred-dollar check, which, after taxes, would amount to a single mortgage payment, not much in the grand scheme of things, but more than he'd earn poring over back issues of the *John Donne Journal* and scrapping, for the forty-thousandth time, his dissertation's opening paragraph. This year, Stash would have to say no to sushi and lobster. He'd have to swallow his pride, get in line at the complimentary Sterno buffet on the second floor of the Ocean Center. He'd also need to charge any and all expenses to the new Discover card, the one Dana had obtained especially for this trip, since the first six months would be interest-free, meaning that if he stuck to a hundred-dollar budget, they could pay off the balance in manageable installments of $16.66. This was a big "if." Last night—their first in Daytona—he and Mike and Matt and Dave and Ty walked five blocks from the Adams Mark Hotel to the Shark Lounge, where they purchased a fifth of Maker's from a pock-faced Russian woman in a leather jumpsuit. They drained the bottle in less than an hour, left the hotel, stumbled through the arcade, heckled a street magician, took a piss off the end of the pier, and returned to the hotel bar where, beneath banners celebrating NASCAR champs, they ordered a round of white russians, which they immediately followed with another round of white russians, and then—come on, seriously, last one!— one more. Before he knew it, Stash had dropped thirty-three dollars. At 1:23 a.m., he ordered a room-service cheeseburger. Price, eleven twenty-two, not including tip. With six days to go, he was forty-two bucks from his limit.

"I dunno," Stash says. "Fifty's pretty steep."

"Nonsense!" Inge says, "you won't find Obey Your Body for less than fifty. But here's the deal. I'm allowed to sell one kit every day for forty. But that's as low as I can go. It's a great bargain. I know you'll be pleased. Touch that thumbnail again. I dare you to say no."

When Stash hands over the Discover card, his eyelid pulses. Inge rings him up, scribbles on the receipt, says, "Remember, they have a two-year guarantee, so if you have any problems, let me know." Stash glances at the receipt: *Come see me again*, it says. Beneath that, a tiny heart, followed by "Inge," followed by four inexplicable symbols: *xxxo*. Then: *p.s. Call me!* Then she wrote all ten digits of her phone number.

Postachian had a history of impulsive splurging; in the last year, he'd purchased a Pink Floyd boxed set ($221.99 at Best Buy) and the ninth edition of *The Anatomy of*

Melancholy, which had been printed in 1800 and boasted solid binding and barely any cover wear ($329 on eBay). As guilt-inducing as those purchases had been, they couldn't touch the psychological burden he now lugs, made manifest not in the form of a new pair of neon-bright running shoes (a splurge he might have justified as an investment in his fitness) but of a semi-transparent bag emblazoned with Amazonian blooms. What's worse is that Stash can't—*won't*—exorcise the bewitching kiosk chick from his mind, keeps unfolding the flirty note, not only to reflect upon the handwriting (idiosyncratically florid, pleasurably legible, a script so undeniably artistic that, had it appeared in a test booklet, would've earned an automatic 8) but also to consider the words "Come see me again," which, although they seemed innocent enough at first, subsequent readings have inspired more provocative interpretations. Why the "me"? Had she only wanted to encourage repeat patronage, she could've written "Come again!" or "Come back." Instead, she'd written "Come see *me*": come again in order to see *me*.

And she'd left her number.

On the next floor, a baby with cornrows eats a gargantuan sandwich cookie; a man in a Bible Man costume—cape, shiny muscle-suit, gladiator mask, foam saber—signs autographs outside Crosses to Bear; and Stash peers over a chrome railing, watching Inge hold court: a group of black guys, with nylon caps suctioned to their heads, oversized jerseys drooping to their knees like shiny nightgowns, have formed a ring around her. One guy rubs his thumbnail, leaps back in disbelief, tries to wipe it off. His friends hoot. He buys four sets.

What Inge writes on his receipt: nada.

"You into her?"

Stash glances over his shoulder. A chubby guy (chin-strap beard, horn-rimmed glasses, hair gelled into spikes) has appeared beside him. He eats a bowl of tiny pastel spheres with a pinky-sized spoon.

"Excuse me?"

"Get in line." Chin-Strap shows him his hands. The nails are clear and shiny. "She's a heartbreaker, brah."

"I don't doubt it," Stash says. "But that's not why I'm watching."

"You into the brothers?"

"What if I were to tell you," Stash says, resting a hand on his waist, "that I'm with a kiosk management company and that I'm conducting some research in your area, as a way of ensuring no discriminatory practices are occurring?"

"Discriminatory practices?"

"You know. Checking to make sure everyone gets treated the same."

Chin-Strap nods. "I'd say that's insane, brah."

"For instance," Stash says, unfolding the receipt, "do the shop-girls of Obey Your Body scribble this little message for everybody?"

Chin-Strap labors to decipher Inge's message. Stash wonders how far he got in school, how he'd do on the A.P. 2? 3? 0? Dash?

Chin-Strap retracts his head violently. "Whoa," he says. "She must've dug you, brah. She didn't write that on *my* receipt."

Nor, Stash will note, as he spends the next half hour watching Inge work the people who stream by her cart, does she write it on anybody else's.

Postachian could end this here. It'd be easy to walk away. Then again, how often has an attractive young woman— and let's be serious, Inge's a 9.5 on a 10 scale if she's anything—supplied her number to him without his asking? Never. Not once. Maybe this was what happened to guys like him, guys who, in their teenage years, sported afro-sized perms and moustaches, guys who once tucked mesh football jerseys into their Z. Cavaricci slacks and fanta-sized about removing Marjorie Whitcomb's turtleneck in the back seat of his IROC: they grew up, gained con-fidence, got married, settled down, and then—and only then—began to exude irresistibly robust pheromones. Now Stash is married, got a kid, another on the way, owns a two-bedroom bungalow less than a mile from downtown Cedar Rapids, which smells, thanks to the Quaker Oats factory, like you're breathing through a bag of cereal. Plus, he's now gainfully—or somewhat gain-fully—employed, by an actual college, albeit a Christian one, not his first choice, but it's work. Not that he doesn't believe in God or loving one's neighbor, but that doesn't mean he has to walk around with a corncob up his ass (which probably accounts for his solid 4.6 out of 5 rating on the Rate My Professor web site, along with comments from former students that say, "I LOVE THIS MAN," or "best professor ever!!!") or that he worries about breaking one of the promises in the school's Purity Pledge, since he appreciates a good swear, attends R-rated movies, downs a few gin-and-tonics every evening, and views circumci-sion as barbaric. Score him points for taking Eucharist, eating the body and drinking the blood of Christ, asking forgiveness for things done and left undone.

Stash flips open his cell. A picture of Gregory—face slathered in cupcake icing, his third b-day—greets him. He shuts it, opens it again, punches the phone number into the keypad. Hits "Send." Breathes, deeply. Crosses his fingers.

"Hello, Inge speaking, who's calling please!"

"Hi, it's Martin Postachian? You sold me a couple—"

"Ah, Martin! How are you, sweetie? Something wrong with your kits?"

"Actually," he says, "it's a little embarrassing. See, I'm not really a mall kinda guy. I walk in and it's like instant disorientation. Sensory overload."

"And?"

"I thought maybe you could straighten me out. Help me, I mean."

"With what?"

"I can't find the shoe store."

"Which one? Shoe Town? Shoe Experience? So Shoe Me?"

"Shoe Town."

"First floor, northeast wing. Need an escort?"

"An escort?"

"I'm due for a break."

"Well . . . ," Stash says."

"Gimme five minutes to lock up my kiosk."

Dana hadn't wanted Postachian to go to Florida. Last February, when the paperwork arrived in the mail, Dana said, You going? Postachian, who'd pledged the previous year would be his last, said, Well, we could really use the money. To which Dana responded, Come on, Martin, it's not about money, it's about getting lit and staying in a two-and-a-half star hotel in a shitty little Florida town, smoking cigars, and ogling tramps in bikinis, to which Postachian replied, Hey, I'm not gonna lie, I'd love to see the guys again, but honestly, I was thinking about how we could use that fourteen hundred. Never mind, Dana said, that I'll be seven months pregnant; what if I went into premature labor, with you more than a thousand miles away? Postachian said, Fine, I won't go. He knew Dana'd be surprised by his lack of fight and that she'd mull things over long enough to feel guilty about depriving him of a paid vacation, which she did. Okay, she'd finally said, you deserve a break, go.

The deal, however, was far from sealed. A couple days after spring semester ended, Dana strolled Gregory around the college campus, which she often did, enjoying the shaded, smooth sidewalks and her stop at the umbrella'd push-cart selling hot pretzels. During this walk, she decided to pop up to Stash's office, where she found a sticky note affixed to his locked door. She recognized the handwriting; it belonged to their babysitter, Mindy Applewhite, who also happened to be Stash's research assistant. The note said, *Tests done, average grade 77.8, see you in Florida,* smiley face. Dana would say later that she'd plucked the note from the door, pocketed it, thought, *That's odd,* and later, *That's totally fucked up,* because Postachian had made no mention of Mindy Applewhite attending the A.P. reading. When she confronted Postachian with this story, he said, Of course I mentioned it, Dana countering with, No you didn't, and Stash saying, It must've slipped my mind, though slipping his mind had been the last thing it'd done. Postachian had been nursing a strange guilt since the moment he suggested the idea to Mindy Applewhite, who was a senior, a young, shapely woman who always dressed to the nines and who, Dana had referred to, on more than one occasion, as "our hot babysitter." A voracious reader, Mindy was also the kind of student who pored over bookshelves, often returning to Postachian's office drunk with enthusiasm for George Herbert metaphysical poetry or Bloom's *The Western Canon* or even the ridiculously dense *Malleus Maleficarum,* a habit which often got them both into trouble, since Stash needed to be working on his dis and she needed to be grading his Lit exams. To say that Postachian had been looking forward to spending time with Mindy was an understatement, and although his infatuation, if one could even call it that, was purely platonic, he couldn't extinguish the little guilt-flames that flared up whenever he imagined sitting next to her on the airport shuttle bus from Orlando to Daytona, or walking beside her on the beach, if only to appreciate the intro-spection the crashing waves might induce, speculating, perhaps, about whether the death of Percy Bysshe Shelley could be blamed on the poet, a less-than-seaworthy ship, bad weather, or marauding pirates. Such conversations, however, were not fated to take place; Mindy Applewhite's grandmother, who lived in San Diego, passed away, and Mindy opted out of the A.P. reading, thus allowing both Dana and Postachian to breathe sighs of relief.

On the down escalator, Postachian flips open his wal-let, to glance at a family photograph, the one taken at Sears last Christmas for $44.97 plus tax, when Gregory wouldn't hold still for the two seconds necessary to get a good shot, because he only wanted to burrow through a basket of the photographer's slobbered-upon stuffed animals—the same photo they'd planned to distribute among family members before they saw how pasty they looked. But Stash doesn't look at the photo, because stick-ered to the interior sleeve is a stack of wrinkled Post-It notes, upon which, during today's scoring, he'd scribbled a few student sentences, including "The most outstand-ing rhetorical strategy William Hazlitt uses is syntax, namely semi-colons, which keeps the reader in suspense," and "It's ironic to pursue something glorious and in the end have it shoot one in the back without notice," and "His death would still be of little consequence despite various commemorative devices erected." By the time he finishes the last one, the escalator's come to an end, and he catches a flash of green—the machine's interior light—through the serrated crack of the last stair as it folds itself under.

"Normally," Inge says, "I take breaks with Lana, from Goth Warehouse, who sits outside, with her Camel Lights and her candy-apple red lighter that says Bitch and blows smoke at mothers and babies and old people. Not that I don't enjoy a cigarette or two when I'm drinking, but I'd prefer not to reek when I'm buffing a potential customer's thumb, you know? If I do stink, I detour through Zilk's and spritz myself with CK One. Which, don't get any ideas, I'm not bisexual. At least not when I'm sober."

They're standing in line at George's Sushi Bar, where, overhead, a cartoon salmon—at least it looks like a salmon, if a salmon could smile toothily and wear a base-ball cap—offers the viewer a chunk of meat it's carved from its hiney. Inge insisted on stopping here, not for sushi, but for iced tea. It's taking forever. Stash swelters in his getup, wonders if he's coming down with a virus or being slowly roasted. This would explain the juice leaking from his armpits.

"What happened to your ring?" Inge asks.

"What ring?"

"The one that allowed that part of your finger not to get tan."

"Oh. Sometimes, it kinda hurts."

"I bet," Inge says, grinning. She grabs his hand, inspects the pale stripe, then flips it over. "Ever had your palm read? Whoa."

"What?"

"See this? Your life line? How it's wavy? That often indicates variable health conditions. Are you very energetic?"

"Somewhat."

"Good. You'll probably be fine. See this?" Inge traces one of her own nails across his palm, glances up, grinning. "When your life line crosses the palm it indicates a life affected by travel. Your life may also be heavily influenced by *imagination*. Am I on the right track so far?"

"Yeah," Stash says. "Is it hot in here? Are you hot? It feels like a hundred degrees."

"See this one? It's your heart line. See how it starts between your index and middle finger? That means you have a tendency to give your heart away easily. A slight disregard of the true meaning of love and its responsibilities are indicated by a heart line like yours."

"Come on," Stash says. "You're making this up."

"Am I?" she asks.

They leave the food court with sweaty cups of Japanese Iced Tea. Inge's still holding his hand, an act so brazen Postachian can't help but feel conspicuous, since it's not the regular, we're-just-a-couple-of-pals-cupping-each-other's-hands hand-holding, it's fingers-interlaced-because-this-means-something hand-holding. Stash could easily let go, but doesn't. In other cultures, people hold hands all the time, even men, and who knows what passes for normal among young Floridians? At this moment, hand-holding seems acceptable. Nothing's happening, right? Or was it? God! What was he? Fifteen? He felt fifteen. He doesn't know jack about this girl, who could be off the hook in terms of instability, chock full of STDs, might even be in possession of a bona fide psychosexual disease, the main symptom of which was she felt compelled to seduce men twice her age as a way of exerting control and/or acting out some fantasy to compensate for the lack of a good childhood and/or a history of sexual abuse, though honestly, aside from being a giant flirt, to him, she seems pretty with it. Still, he has no idea where she'd fall age-wise, except that she's younger, maybe way younger, something to keep in mind, since if she's sixteen, he could be toast from a legal standpoint, and even if she's eighteen, or twenty-two, what could they possible have in common, unless it turns out that she's truly head-over-heels for him? Which is unlikely. But still.

"Wait," Inge says. She comes to a halt, whiplashing Stash to her side. "Holy crap," she says. "Don't move."

"What is it?"

"See that guy?"

"Which one?"

"The one with the spikes on his head."

"Chin-Strap?"

"Huh?"

"Chin-strap beard."

"Yeah. Two weeks ago, I buffed his thumbnail. He's been stalking me ever since. He tries to time his breaks with mine. F-ing sicko."

"You want me to talk to him?"

"*No*. Don't even engage."

Where can a young woman and a man approaching middle age find solace from a punkish stalker? Where else but Willard's? Not in the Home section. Bypass the Home section, with its toasters and mini-jukeboxes and comforters and trays of martini glasses. Skip the perfume counter; sidestep decapitated, Polo-wearing mannequins and head directly toward Women's Undergarments.

"Still there?" Inge whispers, fondling a tiger-print thong.

"Can't see him," Stash says.

"You folks need help?" a woman asks. Leathery face, purplish 'do.

"Yes ma'am," Inge says. "We're looking for something, I don't know, sexy? Yes. We want the sexiest thing you've got."

"I can show you some of our most popular outfits."

Outfits, Stash thinks. *Outfits?*

"What do you think?" Inge asks. She holds a lacy bikini top against her chest. "I'm gonna try it on. Keep an eye out."

•

Postachian has this fantasy—or, not fantasy, since fantasy implies that whatever he's imagining would actually be desirable, more like a possible scenario that occasionally pops into his mind, a sort of "what if" moment when he imagines his family has succumbed to a terrible accident, an automobile crash, say, where his airbag had deployed and Dana's hadn't, and Gregory's car seat went flying because it hadn't been adequately strapped down, despite the fact that Dana had told him a million times to check it, and sometimes he adjusted it and sometimes merely pretended to, because it took a lot of work to pull those straps as tight as the initial seat-checker at the hospital had instructed them to do when they'd first brought Gregory home. Anyway, he's the sole survivor, dragging himself across asphalt littered with shimmering chunks of windshield glass, and Dana's slumped in the passenger's seat, and his son's—well, he usually skips the gory details, preferring to take an imaginary dive into the paralytic shock that would accompany the realization that they're gone forever, a fact that'd shape the rest of his days and crown him with an aura of the Tragic, the lost family members achieving immediate sainthood in the hierarchy of his head, to be worshipped and endlessly contemplated as he wandered the Earth, barely squeaking by on Dana's life insurance funds, meeting other desperate souls, maybe even someone like Inge, who'd find his suffering fascinatingly incomprehensible.

At that point, it might be okay to entertain a scene like the one unfolding now, which, to be honest, he's also considered, i.e., what it would be like to get down with someone else. Supposing Dana gave him a chance to justify his actions, he'd probably try to convince her that it wasn't personal, just something that happened, that hurting Dana or Gregory or the unborn child was the furthest thing from his mind, to which Dana would reply, Are you fucking kidding me? *Nothing personal?* Screwing around with a teenage nail-buffer is *nothing personal?* You're absolutely right, he'd say. I can totally see your point, he'd add, but it'd be too late for seeing other people's points, so he'd have to resort to honesty, and try to explain that all he'd sought was to transcend, for a few moments, the confines of his body, which of course was utterly selfish and wholly indefensible, but, Come on, Dana, don't tell me you haven't fantasized about that? And she'd say, No, Martin, actually I haven't, and he'd say, Well, imagine this, your body athrob with desire, pumped to capacity with adrenaline, totally amped, you're like some sort of pulsing conquistador, or whatever, there's no word for someone like you, who's attracted the attention of someone who seems to want your bod and nothing else, don't you think you'd at least be tempted to indulge the desires of your heart and, drunk with the terror of losing it all, surrender yourself to a state of unadulterated carnality?

Standing outside the changing room, Stash hopes the invitation won't come. The door opens, and Inge, wearing a thong and bikini top, her flesh goose-pimpling in the chilled department store air, whispers, "Com'ere," and he does, and then, as she latches the door shut, "Hurry, we don't have much time." He's trying, but it's not easy. For one thing, there's not much space. Plus, he's trembling, unsure how to operate his body. Breast heaving, blazer shed, he undoes a waistcoat button.

"Wait," Inge says. "Leave that on."

Stash nods. At this point, he's willing to do whatever it takes to get through this, go on with the rest of his life.

"Ah!" Inge says, shaking her head when he reaches for his belt buckle. Her foot—cold, bare, sticky—grazes his hand. "Me first." She wiggles her toes. Unlike her nails, they've not been polished to a glassy sheen. "Start here."

"With—"

"Yes," Inge says, biting her bottom lip.

Whatever, Stash thinks. He squeezes her foot. Having never been a foot man, per se, he opens his mouth, through which he now breathes, in order to keep himself from smelling whatever might be living beneath the toenails. His tongue skims the bottom of her big toe, and oh! She retracts, as if stung.

"What?"

Inge mashes a finger against her lips.

Stash freezes. He listens. Then hears it: a knock.

Stash clears his throat. "Occupied," he says.

"Open the door please. This is Security."

Stash nods, directing Inge behind the door, unlatches the bolt.

It's Chin-Strap. Wearing sunglasses.

"You mind?" Stash replies.

"Actually," Chin-Strap says, "I do." He places a fist against the door. "Why don't you go ahead and open all the way."

"Listen—" Stash says.

"No need to explain. Personally, I don't want to know. But I do want to ask you something. Let's say something terrible happens to you today. Not that it has to, but who knows? Let's say, for argument's sake, it just does. I don't know, maybe some insane guy comes out of nowhere, pulls a gun from the back of his pants, unloads the clip into your face. Bam. Game over. Know for a fact where you'd end up?"

Stash glances back at Inge, with a face like, is this guy on crack? Inge, who's stuffed herself into the corner, says, "Well?"

"It's an easy question," Chin-Strap says.

"I guess it depends," Stash replies.

"It does," Chin-Strap says. "and it doesn't. Only two answers I know of."

"Let's put it this way," Inge says. She crosses her arms, each hand gripping one of her bare arms. "On a scale of one to ten, how on fire for God are you?"

Stash blinks. No way, he thinks. A setup?

"Seriously," Chin-Strap says. "This is a serious question. Imagine if you had to grade yourself, had to give yourself a score, any number, one through ten, where do you think you'd lie?"

Stash's thoughts dart like a fish in a bowl. "If it's money you want," he says.

Inge shakes her head.

"Our goal," Chin-Strap says, "is to make God's kingdom greater, and it will be infinitely greater even if we save just one person. And whether or not you know it, when you stepped into that changing room, you stepped into the next phase of your life. What I'm saying is, I know a broken man when I see one. I came from broken men. I, myself, was a broken man before I came to the Lord. All I want to know is, are you interested? If so, just say it: Lord, I'm interested."

"You don't have to say it out loud," Inge says. "You can totally say it in your head."

Stash blinks.

"Are you saying it in your head?"

He is and he isn't. He nods.

"Good," Inge says.

"Barry," Chin-Strap says, offering his hand.

"Martin," Stash says.

"Martin, now comes the part where we say a prayer for you?"

Stash shakes his head, but Barry pulls him down to kneel. They hold hands, though this time, cupped palm to palm. Never, Stash thinks, has a floor been harder.

"Lord," Chin-Strap says, "we want to thank You for this opportunity to be here. We thank You for softening the heart of Inge's father and for opening up the doors of the Gehenna Mall for Your use. But Lord, we're most thankful for Martin, who You sent here for a reason today, and who we know You love more than we could fathom. Lord, only You know Martin's heart, only You know the workings of his soul, which You personally wove in his mother's womb. You knew him before he had a name and You knew he'd come here today, that he'd end up right here, on his knees, which we know isn't easy, but that's how You roll, Lord, You're a jealous God and want obedience. So now we'd just like to thank You for the blessing of salvation . . . "

As the World's Longest Prayer unfolds, Stash opens his eyes. Inge doesn't peek, not even once, only nods with furrowed brow and whispers "Amen" intermittently. He wants to think, How juvenile, or, What a bitch, but scorn, at this point, seems irrelevant. In her head, he guesses, she's sacrificed herself for a cause larger than anyone can imagine. Plus, it's hard to condemn her mid-prayer, her face resembling that of someone who's dreaming an intensely serious dream, an expression he sees sometimes on Gregory's face, when Stash comes in to straighten his covers and falls in love with him all over again, despite the fact that he'd spent the afternoon drawing on the wall with permanent marker. When Inge bites her lip now and nods fervently, he imagines this is the expression he might've seen if what seemed to be on the verge of happening in the changing room had actually taken place, which, Jesus, what a thing to think during someone's prayer. He feels something then, not exactly a conviction, but a sort of acknowledgment: yes, his nature is monstrous, and yes, he needs forgiveness; he's a man who, if

he had any balls whatsoever, would tell Dana this whole
story, or at least parts of it. So as Chin-Strap drones on,
Postachian begins composing a possible speech in his
head, a sort of prelude to giving his wife the manicure kit,
something along the lines of, Okay, I know you're going
to be skeptical, may think I went too far, but I got you
a little something in Florida, and you have to promise
not to say anything until I'm finished showing you how
it works. At that point, he'd take her hand in his, remove
the block, and begin buffing, like Inge had done, the blue
side first, then gray, then white. He tries to imagine Dana
saying, Wow, that's amazing, or, What a transformation,
but he knows she probably won't be impressed, won't give
a hoot about making her fingernails shine, though she'll
definitely want to know how much he paid for the whole
thing, and so it won't seem like that big of a deal, he'll
give her a number much lower than the actual price,
maybe twenty, maybe fifteen, reminding himself to keep
an eye out for the mail, to reach the credit card state-
ment before she does, write a check for the minimum balance, then file that bad boy away. Because even though
he knows it's deceptive to conceal the evidence of his poor
decision-making, it's much better to launch a pre-emptive
attack against marital strife, since the last thing Stash
wants to do is argue. He can already see Dana jabbing a
finger at the phrase OBEY YOUR BODY on the Visa state-
ment, can hear her asking questions, like, Wait, Martin,
hold up, what's this here? To which he might say, Huh,
and That doesn't make sense, and They must have over-
charged me. Of course, then Dana would want to know
who *they* were and so Stash—in an effort to remain at
least partially honest—might say, Not *they*. *She*. Some
weird kiosk girl as a mall in Daytona, her name was Inge,
I think, maybe I should call the number here and check.
At this point, Dana's eyes might narrow, she might fold

her arms over her chest and say, Inge, huh? and Was she cute? On a scale of one to ten, how hot was she? Because of course she would ask that. And even though Stash should know from experience that it's best to come clean in these situations, and that Dana actually admires it when he has the guts to confess that he's done something utterly moronic, he's also not particularly fond of admitting when he's wrong, prefers to hunker down in his alternate version of reality as long as possible, which means that in this particular situation he might try to change the terms of the argument by calling into question the very existence of Dana's proposed rating system, arguing that such methods of evaluation and "hotness factors" represent the products of a relentlessly patriarchal society that objectifies and demeans women by valuing them merely for their physical appearance. To which Dana would then almost assuredly say, Don't patronize me, Martin. You've got a number in your head. Why don't you just go ahead and tell me what it is? There'd be no way around it then. She'd know a lie by the look on his face or the tone of his voice. He'd have to say the real number. Then, like a secret code, it would open a door, granting access to a room they would rather not visit. And at that point there'd be no turning back. They'd sworn their solemn vows. They'd pledged to be faithful partners, in sickness and in health; to cherish one another as long as they both had breath. They'd clasp one another's hands, launch their silent prayers, and then they'd walk inside.

Gateway to Paradise

-+->-<-+-

"I THOUGHT he wasn't supposed to be home," Jaybird said. He squeezed the steering wheel with both hands and eyeballed the minivan parked in front of a faded pink singlewide. If Gene Holcomb had blown any of his lottery winnings, he'd not spent a dime updating his mode of transportation. The hubcaps on his minivan were gone. The busted passenger-side window had been replaced with a garbage bag. The plastic bulged like a damaged lung taking in air.

"He claimed he had prayer meeting at seven," Riley replied. When she'd called him the week before, she said she'd like to stop by sometime and, you know, catch up. He'd said that'd be nice, and that she should come any night but Wednesday. Wednesday was his church night.

It was half past seven now. On a Wednesday.

Jaybird directed a drool-string into a Coke bottle. He stomped a pedal to engage the parking brake, killed the engine.

"Guess a man like him can't be trusted," he said.

"He's not all bad," Riley muttered.

Rain splatted briefly against the windshield, as though something above had spat on them. With a thumb and forefinger, Jaybird squeezed his nostrils shut, then attempted to suck air through his nose, forcing the holes closed. It was something he did now and again. Said it helped him clear his head.

"We could come back later," Riley suggested. She rubbed her palms on her jeans, fanned air through her shirt. The car's vents blasted frigid wind. Still, she was sweating.

Jaybird shook his head. "We've already gone to all this trouble. I say we go with Plan B."

Jaw clenched, Riley unbuckled her seat belt. She wasn't crazy about Plan B. Plan A was non-confrontational, in part because they'd be dealing with an empty trailer. No masks. No weapons. Plan B was a different beast entirely, as evidenced by the firearm that Jaybird had removed from the glove box and now set on the seat between them. A .38 Special.

"I dunno," she said.

"What's there to know?" Jaybird said. He tossed a pair of gardening gloves—the undersides pebbled with tiny rubber circles, to help the wearer better grip his chosen implement—onto Riley's lap, then stretched a ski mask over his head. "Don't think about it. Just do like we said. Be a machine."

"Right," Riley said. "A machine."

It sounded phony. Like something Coach West would say when he wanted to trick her into believing that launching a barrage of threes could reverse a blowout. Only they weren't here to reduce any deficits; they were here to create one. Riley stuffed her head into the mask. Her face itched. She was hot. She grabbed the handle to open her door, felt her heartbeat in the tips of her fingers.

•

Uncle Gene wasn't Riley's uncle; he was her second cousin once removed, thirty-six years her senior. Years before, Riley's mother had been hospitalized for a kidney ailment, and Riley had spent a week under the care of Aunt Wanda and Uncle Gene. They'd let Riley skip her bath and use real scissors to cut up the funny pages. They'd let her dip Twinkies in chocolate milk and eat baloney sandwiches on white bread. One night, when Aunt Wanda was popping corn in the kitchen, Uncle Gene asked Riley if she didn't want a horsey ride. She hopped on his knee; he looped a finger through a belt loop of her jeans. His leg vibrated. Then the tickling began. Only it wasn't just tickling. It was like some kind of game. He kept asking, "Where's that ol' pocketbook?" Riley wanted to tell him she didn't have a pocketbook but she couldn't breathe. He'd say, "Is this it?" and jab a finger in her armpit or under her chin. "How about here?" he'd say. "Or here?" Then he said, "I think I found it. Yessiree. I think I found that ol' pocketbook." His hand slipped in—and then out of—the front of her underwear.

It'd made Riley feel funny, but not bad—at least not until years later, when, during a sleepover, she'd told the story to Amber Pullium who claimed it was the totally grossest thing she'd ever heard. Was it? Riley wondered. She couldn't even prove it'd happened. Her own mother thought she must've been mixed up. Did Riley think her own mother would leave her little girl with people who couldn't be trusted? Uncle Gene, her mother insisted, had been nothing but nice. And then Aunt Wanda had gone and left him for a retarded boy from Hanging Dog. If anybody deserved to win something, Riley's mother had said, it was Gene Holcomb.

The handle refused to turn. Jaybird kicked the door twice with the heel of his boot. The aluminum dented

and the door swung open. A walleyed Chihuahua-mix
ran in circles, yapping. It resembled a toy in the throes
of malfunction.

Uncle Gene, wearing skivvies and an unsnapped cowboy shirt, gripped the arms of his recliner as if preparing
for liftoff. His nose was threaded with broken blood ves-
sels. Grayish splotches appeared on his forehead. His bare
legs looked pathetically skinny, sprigs of hair appearing
around his kneecaps like little strings of plant life.

"Don't get up," Jaybird said. He pointed the .38 at Gene.
"In fact, don't move."

Uncle Gene obeyed. A stainless steel mixing bowl
rested on his lap. Inside: a fresh hot fudge sundae, com-
plete with a mountain of Reddi-wip and a maraschino
cherry. The whipped cream shivered. The room flickered
with light. A TV displayed a white-haired woman smiling
serenely while riding a bicycle. A voiceover listed the side
effects of a mood-altering pharmaceutical, the majority
of which were drowned out by Uncle Gene's yapping dog.

There was no doubt that Riley had the steadier hand.
Whenever they tied empty gallon milk jugs to tree limbs
behind Jaybird's house and took turns shooting, she out-
performed him every time; after finishing her rounds,
every container would be swaying. But she'd made it clear
that she wouldn't point a gun at anybody, especially one
that Jaybird insisted stay loaded. There was no way to
know what they might be walking into, he'd said.

Riley's job, then, was to locate the lottery money. If
she couldn't find it within ten minutes, they'd split. In
situations like this, Jaybird had claimed, it was best not
to linger. At least, that was his sense of it, and Riley
had deferred to his intuition. Aside from snitching the
occasional grape in the grocery store, she'd never sto-
len anything, though, on several occasions, she'd inad-
vertently served as accessory, having accompanied

Tyra Needles—a girl who'd since been saved at Grace Baptist—when she'd exited Walmart with an armful of five-dollar DVDs, and had been rolling in the same girl's Pathfinder when she'd peeled rubber out of an Amoco station without paying for gas.

Riley and Jaybird had agreed there was no need to tear the place apart. With this in mind, she removed—then replaced—Uncle Gene's couch cushions one at a time. She found popcorn shards, a few pennies, a pencil worn down to its nub, and a plastic steak that wheezed when she squeezed it. She tossed the steak at the dog, who yelped, jumped backwards, then cautiously approached it, sniffing.

"If y'all tell me what you're looking for . . . ," Gene said, his voice rasping.

"Are you fucking crazy!" Jaybird cocked the gun. "Flinch and I'll blast your lungs out!"

"Jesus," Riley whispered.

"Shut up!" Jaybird yelled. He pointed a finger at Riley.

Riley wasn't supposed to talk, on the off chance that Uncle Gene might recognize her voice. She raised her hands apologetically. The phrase *my bad* entered her head—one that she'd used in high school, when setting an ineffective screen for a pick and roll. But it wasn't really her bad. She'd only whispered. She didn't deserve to be yelled at, and there was no point in scaring Uncle Gene. There had been nothing in Plan B about acting like an asshole, or even pretending to act like an asshole. She flipped open her phone. Three and a half minutes had elapsed.

In another life—one she sometimes allowed herself to imagine—Riley had kept playing basketball. She'd said yes to a scholarship at Western. She'd stuffed her clothes into trash bags, packed a laundry basket with shoes and sheets and a desk lamp and a clock radio, driven herself

to school in her mom's muffler-less hatchback. She'd
roomed with one of her former teammates—a black girl
who was six and a half feet tall. The whole team wore
matching metallic purple warm-up suits that swished
when they walked. There'd been 5 a.m. workouts, weights
to lift, suicides to run. She'd gone to parties; she'd danced
to the music of foul-mouthed R&B singers. She'd slept
on buses, eaten chicken breasts and mashed potatoes in
vast dining halls. She'd run the offense, made buzzer-
beating threes. She'd juked a UConn player so hard that
the player had injured herself. She'd had her nose busted.
Her ankle taped. She'd set a school record for career
assists. Given post-game interviews. Posed beside giant
cardboard checks. Autographed shoes.

But Riley had not said yes to basketball. After a decade
of playing on Midget and Mite and Junior Varsity and
Varsity teams, she'd said no. No to practices, to crunches,
laps and free throws, and lonely hours shooting threes.
More importantly, she'd also said no to school. It wasn't
like she had a special zeal for cashiering or the shame-
less parade of humanity her register attracted on a daily
basis, but at least she didn't have homework. When she
was done working she was done for the day. Someday,
she'd find a job that would let her labor behind the scenes:
a personal assistant, a chef, a housekeeper, whatever. She
needed only to never wear makeup or heels. Clothing-
wise she preferred hoodies and jeans, bright high tops.
Hair ponytailed or—someday, if she ever had the guts to
cut it—short like a boy's, with bangs and a fade in back
that, when she rubbed it, would feel like the soft bristles
of a clean paintbrush.

Nothing in the wood stove but ashes, a charred log, and a
pile of cigarette butts. Nothing in the bookcase but crossword puzzle workbooks and a framed photograph of Dolly

Parton signed, "To Gene, with Love, Dolly." Nothing in the closet but a carpet sweeper, half a dozen flannel shirts, and a forlorn-looking Falcons parka. Uncle Gene's house was a storehouse of things nobody'd ever want. A Museum of Lonesome Things.

In the bedroom, Riley slid the mask onto her forehead, desperate for fresh air. Only the air smelled like dog piss and old shoes. She breathed through her mouth as she opened drawers, dug through piles of yellowed tube socks and Fruit of the Loom underpants and T-shirts bearing Atlanta Braves insignias. She spotted a thick Bible sitting on a bedside table, next to a lamp in the shape of a deer. Imagining that the middle of the book might've been cut out so as to stow treasure inside, she opened it. The book was intact. Pages had been marked up, passages highlighted. On page 778, she read a sentence a shaky hand had blazed yellow: "A sword, a sword, drawn for the slaughter, polished to consume and to flash like lightning!" She got down on the floor, flipped open her phone and aimed its light under the bed. Half crushed soda cans, dust bunnies, a crumpled tissue, and a little pamphlet that asked, "Are Roman Catholics Christians?"

She donned her mask. She wondered what prayers Uncle Gene, even now, might be lifting to Heaven.

In the freezer, nestled between a box of fish sticks and a tub of Rocky Road, Riley found a gray plastic bag, upon which the words "True Value" had been printed. Inside, there were four stacks of hundred-dollar bills. Hundreds of hundreds. She'd never seen so many. That they were bound so thickly boggled her mind, thwarted any attempts to make a preliminary count. She opened her phone, checked the time. Seven minutes and thirty-one seconds had elapsed. She lifted her hoodie, stuffed the bag down her underpants. The plastic was cold there, against her flesh. The frosted sack produced a sort of prickling glow. She rearranged her hoodie. Felt decidedly giddy. Light on her feet. Mobile. Her stomach growled. She glanced around the kitchen. An outdated wall calendar showed a photo of a hound dog wearing sunglasses. Above the sink, gnats pulsed. She stuck a finger inside a jar of Marshmallow Fluff, swiped a congratulatory glob into her mouth. It was a celebration, she thought. The first, she assumed, of many.

From the living room, Jaybird yelled a single word: "Motherfucker!"

A pop sounded. Everything went quiet.

Riley froze. "Jaybird?" she said, in a loud whisper.

"He moved," Jaybird called out.

"Then what?" she said. She stood perfectly still, as if Uncle Gene's welfare depended on it.

"I pulled the trigger."

She took a step forward. The bag in her pants rustled.

"But you didn't shoot him, though. Right?"

"Well," Jaybird said, "he didn't shoot himself."

Riley dropped the jar. It rolled across the linoleum. The dog, who has stopped barking with the pop, now went back to frenzied yelping.

Jaybird appeared in the doorway. "You might not wanna go in there," he said. His eyes bulged inside the ski mask. She tried to lunge past him. He grabbed her arm.

"Let go," Riley said.

"Suit yourself."

Riley slid her mask back on and approached Uncle Gene's chair. The dog was going bananas, going hoarse. Streams of blood—thick and arterial—trickled from Uncle's Gene's mouth and nose. A hand twitched near the wound in his chest, as if to confirm it was actually there. His lips made an O-shape. He did not blink. The dog sniffed the man's shoe, then huddled beside it, shivering.

Smoke-tendrils dispersed through the air. On the wall, the second hand on a slab of wood continued its rotations.

"Oh my God," Riley said.

"At least he ain't suffering," Jaybird said. He shoved the gun into his jeans.

"Are you kidding me?" Riley said. "He's bleeding from his fucking mouth!"

"That's just the lungs filling with blood, then sending it up and out."

"Just?"

"A side effect of getting shot in the heart."

"How do you even *know* that?"

"It's not like it's a secret. Any fool can look it up."

"This is so fucked," Riley said. She patted the legs of her jeans, trying to locate her phone. "I'm calling 911."

"Be my guest," Jaybird said. "While you're at it, call the cops, too. And the humane society. That little piece of shit's gonna need a new home."

Jaybird had claimed he'd never orchestrated a heist, but in the case of Gene Holcomb it seemed pretty straightforward. If it was true what Riley's mom had heard from a teller at Citizens Bank that the man had been making sizable withdrawals on a weekly basis—presumably so he could keep a nice stack of cash at home—they'd just figure out when he wasn't around, break in, and take a little bit for themselves. Gene had more than he knew what to do with already, and he had more checks coming. So it wouldn't be like they'd be putting any kind of actual hurt on him. Plus, from Jaybird's perspective, Uncle Gene owed Riley reparations for the undue psychological stress he'd inflicted.

"That's not how I'd put it," Riley had said.

"Of course you wouldn't," Jaybird had explained. "Who wants to think of themselves as a victim? You've probably spent your whole life repressing that shit. Now you gotta chance to reclaim some power."

Riley hadn't been completely sold on the idea, but she had few doubts that Jaybird could plan and execute a successful robbery. She'd watched him replace a carburetor, brew his own beer, pick the master lock at her mom's self-storage facility when they'd lost the key. Once, she'd observed him grip the sides of a gutter and walk right up the side of a wall, then scramble onto the roof, just to prove he could. He'd convinced Riley that contraception was a conspiracy concocted by capitalist society, as evidenced by its insistence on selling you rubbers that'd numb your dick and pills that'd give you titty cancer. Furthermore, he'd promised that if they avoided each other on the days she ovulated, they'd be good to go. And—so far—they had been.

Now, Riley lifted a vinyl toilet seat with her foot and vomited into the bowl. She studied the cloudy liquid as if it might deliver a message. The unfurling tendrils resembled a miniature universe expanding, a galaxy that had yet to produce intelligent life. Her forehead was sweaty; she dabbed it with a square of toilet paper. Uncle Gene had picked out this paper from all the others, had taken care to place it on the roller. Surely, he had not thought it'd be the last time he'd ever do this.

In another part of the house, Jaybird was going apeshit. She could hear stuff breaking. Cabinet doors slamming. She pictured his boot crushing the oven window. A smashed TV screen. Broken curtain rods, ruined blinds. The clatter of ice cubes on linoleum. It was as if he were punishing Gene's home for failing to reveal its secrets.

It had scared her at first, which was why she stayed locked in the bathroom; she didn't want to be subsumed by his anger—a storm she'd never had to weather. This was, after all, the man who took care, when a wasp found its way inside his house, to trap it—using a sheet of paper and a glass—and then toss it outside.

She froze when he banged on the door.

"What the hell are you doing in there?" he yelled.

"What do you think I'm doing?" she yelled back. She didn't like the tone of his voice, as if there might be consequences —a punishment of some kind—if she didn't hurry.

"I don't know. That's why I'm asking."

"I'm *using* the *bathroom*," she said.

"Well, hurry up!"

"I'm *trying!*" she yelled back.

She switched on the faucet. She needed a second to think. She shoved a hand into her pants, to resituate the bag, rearrange the bulge, even it out. Because Jaybird couldn't know about it. Not yet. Not in the state he was in. You couldn't reward somebody who'd made such a bad mistake. Assuming it even was a mistake. Assuming he hadn't planned to shoot Gene from the very beginning. It was terrible to think Jaybird couldn't be trusted, but she couldn't be too careful. They were in this mess together. And the less crazy she could make it, the better off they'd be. Protect the money, get somewhere safe, pray Jaybird would come to his senses and that she wouldn't somehow re-ignite the flame of his anger. Then maybe there was still a chance everything could turn out okay.

She yanked the bottom of her hoodie over the bulge in her pants. Studied her reflection in the mirror over the sink. Told herself she looked more or less normal for somebody who'd just stared down a dead man and was toting his loot in her pants.

She opened the door. In the next room, Jaybird was leaning an elbow against the wall, tapping the gun barrel absentmindedly against his forehead. She noted a constellation of tiny red blotches on his shirt. *Uncle Gene's blood.* She shut her eyes.

"Find anything?" she said.

Jaybird turned toward her. "No." He chewed on his bottom lip. "Didn't find shit." His eyes darted, as if he was considering his next move.

"So now what?"

"We get the hell outta here," Jaybird said. He sniffed long and hard.

"What about . . ." Riley nodded in the direction of Uncle Gene.

"What about him?"

"I dunno, Jaybird. It's not like I've ever been in this situation before."

"I say leave him the way he is."

The way he is, Riley thought. A short while ago, the man had pulsed with life. Now, thanks to a plan she'd helped implement, he was a body, upon whose lap a dessert would melt. She prayed for the universe to reverse time. To give them another chance to get it right. She wanted a do-over. The universe refused to comply.

It'd been Jaybird's idea to tell people they were leaving town the day before—that way they'd have an alibi. They'd said goodbye to Riley's mother, driven to Waynesville, rented a Ford Escort, checked into a Knight's Inn, gotten up the next morning and taken the rental (to ensure they wouldn't be recognized) to Uncle Gene's. Now, they were headed back to exchange vehicles. After that, they'd head north, to Maine, where Jaybird's cousin's girlfriend's dad owned a seaside restaurant and had promised them work. If they liked it there, who knew? They might stay.

The problem with departures, Riley thought, was that somebody got left behind. In this case, it was her mom. The woman was almost blind, even with her glasses. She survived on a disability check, tended to the plastic flowers in the gravel orbiting the duplex, smoked Mistys, and waited for the mail. In the evenings, she watched TV with a magnifying glass and shouted letters at *Wheel of Fortune*. Why, oh why, would anyone ever buy a vowel? She—Riley's mother—was sure there was some sort of vowel-buying conspiracy afoot. Then again, her mother believed there were conspiracies everywhere. The entirety of human life was the product of a cosmic conspiracy between the forces of good and evil. At least that's what she'd learned by reading the Book of Revelation with the help of an online Bible study series.

But then there were her mom's impromptu visits to McDonald's, where, if things were slow, she would dunk an Apple Pie into her coffee and call out clues from a jumbo-sized crossword puzzle book while Riley wiped tables. Riley would miss this. She'd miss their walks after dark, trying to see into the lives of others in houses whose shades hadn't been pulled. She'd miss telling her mother goodnight and her mother's hand the next morning, rubbing Riley's back softly to wake her.

"Maine, huh," Riley's mother had said, when Riley and Jaybird had broken the news. Riley had made Fettuccine Alfredo, her mother's favorite meal, with a little side salad of iceberg drizzled with Catalina dressing, and a mug of white wine. "Never been to Maine myself," her mother added.

"We'll bring you back something nice," Jaybird said. He got up for seconds, then bent to kiss Riley's mom's forehead. In return, the woman made a smooching sound. She was not a person who kissed back.

Until recently, Riley had known next to nothing about Maine. The state had simply been the head of the bloated dragon shape that was America. Maine's name seemed to betray itself. It was not central. As the country's

northernmost state on its eastern side, it could be said to
stand at something of a remove. According to the pictures
they'd viewed on the Internet, it was clean and bright and a
little forlorn. It had affably pompous lighthouses guarding
rocky outcroppings. It had blood-red barns. In winter, it had
snowdrifts and evergreens and burly steeds pulling sleighs.
Maybe, Riley had thought, Maine was the place to be.

"Isn't that where what's-his-name's from?" Riley's
mother asked. "You know. That writer who writes all the
gore."

"Stephen King?" Jaybird said.

"That's him. He always looked evil to me."

"Lots of people look evil to you," Riley said. She reached
a hand into her hoodie, to resituate her old Wildcats jersey: #19. She'd never been superstitious outside of basketball, but it did help to think of what she and Jaybird were
about to do as a game. She was wearing her Jordans,
too. The black ones, with the pink tongue and orange silhouette. Laced up for the first time in she didn't know
how long.

"But him especially," her mother said. "He looks like
he's done somebody some damage."

"It's that long upper lip," Jaybird offered.

Riley's mother chewed and nodded. She slugged the
last of her wine, poured herself an unprecedented second
cup. "Well," she said, "keep me posted. And for the love of
Pete, don't pull over at any rest stops. Nothing good has
ever happened at a rest stop. Of that I'm one hundred percent convinced."

The woman reached out her hand. Riley squeezed it,
but couldn't look her mother in the eye; she feared she
might give something away. Instead, she stared out the
front window, where green ridges rose in the distance:
steep mountains whose banks were thicketed with briars
and rhododendron brakes so dense that even at high noon

only the slenderest flames of sunlight slithered along the forest floor. People here liked to say there was no prettier valley. But when Riley considered the jagged-tipped rim that encircled her, she imagined a vast cauldron—one that, on summer days like this, might as well be slow-cooking to death every person inside.

"I got something to confess," Jaybird said. They were headed to the motel in the rental. A bug smacked the windshield, left an incandescent smudge. Jaybird flicked the turn signal. A stream of fluid spurted against the glass. Wipers half-erased the smear. It looked like the old Jaybird was back. He steered using the underside of his wrist, dribbled dip-spit into a bottle.

"About what?" Riley said.

"Ol' Gene," Jaybird replied. Weirdly, the expression on his face was whimsical, as if he were remembering the first deer he'd killed.

"Okay."

"He didn't move."

"What do you mean?"

"I mean he just sat there. Still as a snake."

"Then why'd you shoot him?"

"I didn't like the way he looked."

"How'd he look?"

"Like somebody who'd diddle his own blood relative and thought he could live to tell about it."

Riley's chest constricted. She couldn't breathe right. Every breath was a little bit short.

"I knew it," she whispered.

"Knew what?"

"You *wanted* to shoot him. From the very beginning you did."

Jaybird squinched up his face. "I wouldn't say want as much as *need*."

Riley shook her head. "You shot him out of pure mean-
ness. For nothing."

Jaybird snorted. "Putting him out of somebody else's
misery's not *nothing*."

"Whose misery?"

"Yours. Mine."

"No, *this* is my misery. You shot Uncle Gene and killed
him. I was there. That makes us . . ." Riley stopped. She
didn't want to say it.

"What."

"Murderers."

"I wouldn't put it that way," Jaybird said. He lifted the
bottle to his mouth and spat.

"Then how would you put it?"

He shrugged. "Not everything needs a name."

Riley leaned her head against the window. She didn't
notice that four lanes had melted to two. Didn't read the
sign across from the First Baptist Church that asked
passersby where they planned to spend eternity. Didn't
see the billboard on the opposite side of the road, the
one that displayed two speech bubbles. One bubble said,
"Dear God please send us someone to cure cancer, AIDS,
etc." The other replied, "I did, but you aborted him."

Her eyes were closed. The plastic bag was warm. Riley
was getting sweaty down there. It was like wearing a
moist, cheap diaper. She pressed hard against her stomach. The plastic stuck and unstuck to her skin. She still
had no idea how much money she was carrying. Only
that not moving the lower half of her body minimized
the chance that the plastic would crackle. Jaybird had
already wondered once what that sound was, and she'd
had to act like it was all in his head.

Outside her window, trees—swallowed by kudzu—
blurred. She cranked a handle, lowered the pane. Now
that she had the money, she realized she couldn't think

of a single thing she wanted to buy. There was nothing she wanted except this, maybe. The sensation of forward motion, of leaving old things behind.

Riley hadn't always liked Jaybird. When she'd first started cashiering, he'd come in and order a number nine minus tartar sauce with a Diet Coke and fries without salt, which meant she'd have to start a new batch, even if there was a pile sitting right there, hot as a heap of coals. It'd been supremely annoying, a ritual she'd performed for a guy who didn't even say thank you. Once, after he'd received his fries, she'd ventured into the dining room to wipe down tables and discovered him alone at a booth. He had little pleated paper cups into which he'd squirted mustard, mayonnaise, and ketchup. He picked up a single fry, salted it, then dunked it into each cup. There was a maddening order to this approach. Riley could barely stand to watch it.

"I don't get it," she'd said. "You ask for fries without salt, then you salt them."

He aimed a heavy-lidded gaze directly at her. "I like 'em fresh."

"Seriously?"

He shrugged. "No. I just get a kick out of watching you make them."

"Kiss my ass."

"You'd like that."

She'd slung her rag at him. She'd aimed for his chest, but it'd slapped him in the face before falling to the floor. "I wouldn't touch you to save my life," she said.

He wiped a hand across his forehead. Resumed eating. "Then I hope it never comes to that," he said, grinning.

He'd subsequently pestered her until she agreed to a Thursday night movie. He'd shown up at the Valleytown Twin Cinema incognito: his usual bandana replaced by an Orioles cap, wearing a pair of glasses and a hooded camouflage sweatshirt. They'd watched a movie whose premise seemed ridiculous, then terrifying: anybody who viewed a cursed videotape would be visited seven days later by a girl whose long wet hair was drawn over her face. It'd happen like this: TVs came to life of their own accord and the resultant static would resolve itself into a shuddering image of an old well in the clearing of a forest. The ghost girl would hoist herself out of the well, then tumble out of the TV.

They'd watched the movie the week before OMC—the Outboard Marine Company—had laid off half its workers, which meant that Riley's mother still had her job working the graveyard shift, which meant that, had Riley gone home, she would've had to sit by herself in the duplex all night, imagining the TV coming inexplicably to life. And she hadn't wanted to be alone.

After the movie, Jaybird had taken her to the house on Grape Creek that he'd recently purchased at a foreclosure auction. In an unfinished room whose windows billowed with tarps, Jaybird assembled a gravity bong. He sawed off the bottom of a plastic three-liter bottle. To the top, he fitted a square of aluminum foil he'd punctured half a dozen times with the sharp end of a pencil, shaping it to make a bowl. He lowered the bottle into a bucket filled with creek water. Then he placed a sparkling budchunk into the foil bowl and lit it. Ever so slowly, he lifted the bottle. "We're creating a vacuum," he said solemnly, as if the thick smoke now curdling into the belly of this plastic container was part of an ancient ritual over which he was presiding. Once the bottle had filled with smoke, Jaybird removed the foil. Following his instruction, Riley lifted the bottle to her lips, pushed the bottle back down, and inhaled. She was so high after one hit she feared her eyeballs might explode. Jaybird gave her a clementine and she observed with fascination the poofs of fragrant mist that rose into the air when she tore into its peel. Jaybird had plugged in his homemade guitar, punched play on a boom box. A cassette spooled a recording of a live song—"A Saucerful of Secrets," Pink Floyd, at Pompeii—into which he threaded a bluesy solo, a speculative string of notes composing a question that could never be answered. Later, he swung a lantern through a rhododendron thicket just beyond his backyard, followed a trail to a springhouse, where, before he kissed her, he'd ladled water into her mouth, as sweet as any she'd ever tasted. She chided herself then for thinking he might be "the one." But it was nice to imagine that she'd found someone good.

At Party Time—a combination grocery store, gas station, and videotape rental facility across the street from the Knight's Inn—Riley glanced at the security camera bolted to the ceiling and wondered if they—if she, in particular—looked guilty, and if guilty people were more aware of security cameras than the non-guilty. The cashier didn't seem to give much of a shit either way. She was a big woman whose bra-less breasts formed massive oblongs beneath her T-shirt, a vast, dress-like garment whose sleeves fell past her elbows and whose front said, "Deal With It." One of the woman's arms was lacerated with scratches.

Half a pizza, topped with desiccated-looking pepperoni, rotated inside a grease-smeared plastic case. Riley reached for a slice. It was flat and dry and stiff. She slid it into a paper bag and stood in line with Jaybird, who bought a case of imported beer, three sacks of beef jerky, and five candy bars.

"Y'uns got me in trouble," the cashier said.

"Oh, yeah?"

"That movie ya'll rented? My granddad saw that one slide in through the slot this morning," the cashier said, nodding at Riley.

Riley glanced at the "Adults Only" sign above a green curtain. Last night, she and Jaybird had slipped behind the curtain and browsed the porn. She'd never seen porn. All the more reason to rent one, Jaybird argued. The film featured beautiful women and ugly, angry-faced men with shaved bodies. They weren't as muscular as she'd imagined, though they were quite definitely endowed. Maybe that was the only thing that mattered. Riley didn't know. The sex they had looked mean. The women gritted their teeth and snarled and frowned and yelled out the names of their genitalia, alternately called each other "baby" and "bitch." One woman slapped the tits of another woman, then sat on her face. Riley didn't know there would be that kind of thing in the movie. She wanted to turn it off, but Jaybird had said, "Hold on a minute. I wanna see how this ends." It'd ended like this: all the ladies had jizz in their hair.

"So?" Jaybird said.

"So," the cashier said, "he didn't think she was eighteen."

"She ain't," Jaybird said. "She's twenty-one."

"She ain't no twenty-one."

"Show her," Jaybird said.

"I don't have to show her shit," Riley said.

The cashier snorted. "Whatever," she said.

Riley pretended to read the door labeled EXIT, which was a regular door of solid wood, not glass. Her pretend reading led to actual reading. Here, on this door, people had tacked notices. One was: "Good guard dog, free, seriously only." One was a prayer list and included the line, "Susie May, Cancer." One of the names—Bo Bryson—on the list had been crossed out. She thought about writing

"Gene Holcomb" in the last empty space but there was no pen, only a length of frayed string taped to the door.

At the Knight's Inn, Jaybird unleashed a voluminous piss-stream into the toilet. Riley unzipped her hoodie, slid the bag of money from her pants. She was afraid to count—to know, for sure, how much was there. The .38 sat on a desk beside a table lamp and a pad of stationery. She tempted herself with the thought that she might snatch it, stuff it down her pants, hoist her backpack, and hightail it out of there. Drive Jaybird's truck back to the rental car place. Obtain a nondescript vehicle. Head west, until she reached a shimmering desert, where she'd lie low in a motel or a rent-a-trailer. Sure, she'd be lonely. She'd miss Jaybird. But she'd be free. Unknown, but more herself. She could spend Uncle Gene's money raising cacti and saving stray animals. The money would be an offering. She could rededicate herself to life.

The toilet flushed.

Too late. She crammed the bag into the bottom of her backpack, beneath layers of socks and shirts and jeans. Maybe, she thought, she could simply forget about it. Out of sight, out of mind, or whatever. She fell onto the bed, aimed the remote at the TV. A gray-haired man—one eyebrow raised—ambled through a shadowy parking garage. Preparing for the unthinkable, he claimed, was the greatest gift anyone could give oneself. Therefore, he continued, everyone—young and old, tall and small, woman and man—should carry a Taser.

Jaybird popped the top on a can of Bud, drank it down in five gulps, crushed the can, tossed it onto the floor, belched, and said, "Hey."

"Yeah?" Riley replied.

"I want you to do something for me."

Riley glanced in his direction. "What," she said, flatly.

She had a pretty good idea what the something would be.
She was prepared—out of spite—to deny it.

"I want you to pretend like you're somebody who ain't
heard about you-know-who."

"You mean Gene?"

Jaybird nodded. He cleared his throat. His eyes wid-
ened. He was, it seemed, getting into character. "Holy
shit," he said. "You hear about ol' Gene Holcomb?"

"No," Riley said. "What?"

"Somebody shot him."

She raised herself onto her elbows. "What?" she said.

Jaybird nodded slowly. Gravely. "Some cold-blooded
motherfucker *shot* him. Right in the heart."

"You're kidding."

"'Fraid not."

"Who did it?"

"Nobody knows."

"Is he okay?"

Jaybird frowned disdainfully. "Hell no, he's not okay!
He's fucking *dead!*"

"Oh my God," Riley said. She placed a hand on her
chest. "Why would anybody shoot Gene?"

"You tell me."

"I wouldn't know."

"Didn't he stick his finger up your cootch?"

"Jesus."

"No. Seriously. I mean, did he or did he not take inde-
cent liberties with you? At the age of *nine.*"

"I can't remember."

On the television, a woman wearing a Spandex body-
suit used a Taser to paralyze a professional cage fighter.
The man in the suit said that anyone could own one for a
price he claimed to be low but, in Riley's opinion, was not.

"You ain't playing right," Jaybird said.

"Well," Riley replied, "you said to pretend."

•

Jaybird snorted. In fifteen minutes, he was asleep on his back. Riley flicked out the light, crawled under covers she hoped weren't swarming with invisible bugs. Above her, lights from passing cars slid like ghosts across the pebbled ceiling. With a thumb and forefinger, she forced her eyes shut, tried to follow the instructions of her coach, who'd supplied a specific strategy for her teammates to employ on the nights they couldn't sleep: imagine draining all your threes.

"What the fuck," Jaybird said. It was morning. He'd already showered and shaved. He started nudging Riley.

The motel room came into focus. An amoeba-shaped stain on the wall stared back at her. *Thank God*, Riley thought. In her most recent dream, Uncle Gene was sitting at a booth in a diner, eating pancakes. He kept mistaking Riley for his waitress. "Could I have some more of these?" he said, and before she could explain, blood would erupt from a hole in his chest. "Oh no," he mumbled, "not again." He'd fumbled with the napkin dispenser, couldn't get any out. Riley had handed him a rag, which he'd stuffed into the hole, but the hole spat the rag out. The hole appeared to have teeth. It was eating Uncle Gene's shirt, sucking the fabric tight against his flabby chest.

"You need to call your mom," Jaybird said. A dollop of shaving cream dangled from an earlobe, then disappeared after he slid a white V-neck over his head. As a rule, Jaybird did not wear clothing with words. Words betrayed one's affiliations, and thus one's identity; he preferred—whenever possible—to stay anonymous. "Tell her we're in Gettysburg. And that we're checking out of the . . . General Lee Manor."

Riley's mom appreciated updates, and had requested that they call her every so often. In preparation for Riley and Jaybird's trip, she'd magneted a map of the United States to her fridge; she intended to trace their progress with an orange highlighter.

"You know she's gonna look that up," Riley said. That was for certain. Riley's mom looked up everything, zoomed in on web pages so tightly that each letter was the size of a half-dollar. How many calories were in a banana? Who was the supreme leader of Iran? How much would somebody pay for an ounce of rubies? Why did people yawn? When was the best time of year to go on a cruise? Any question that occurred to her, whether or not the answer would ever prove helpful, she typed into a search engine. It was a quality that Jaybird—who nursed his own streak of insatiable curiosity—admired.

"Let her," Jaybird said. "It's an actual place. We'll be there tomorrow for real, if you can get your ass outta that bed."

"But what do I say?"

"Whatever you want."

"At least tell me something we're supposed to've seen."

"Shit. I don't know. Some Civil War type shit. A band of re-enactors preparing for battle. Tents and muskets. Or whatever the fuck they used."

Riley dialed her mother's number.

"Hello?"

"Mama?"

"'Bout time you called."

"We drove all night."

"That was a stupid thing to do."

"We weren't tired."

"Bodies need rest. A good eight hours, at *least*."

"We're in Gettysburg," Riley said.

"Huh," her mother replied.

"We saw some re-enactors."

"What were they re-enacting?"

Riley moved the mouthpiece from her mouth to her neck. "What were they re-enacting," she whispered.

Jaybird studied his left hand carefully. With a pair of scissors from a Swiss Army Knife, he clipped a flap of dead skin from an index finger and said, "Pearl Harbor."

Riley rolled her eyes. "They never said," she mumbled.

"Don't let Jaybird drive the whole way," her mother instructed. "Driver fatigue is a real thing, you know. Give that man a break once in a while."

Riley promised she would. She said goodbye and hung up. *They haven't found him*, she thought. It would've been the first thing out of her mother's mouth. Uncle Gene was still sitting there—dead—in his chair. Flies—fat and green, the kind that looked metallic, like tiny robots— were probably buzzing around his wound, exiting his nose-holes, laying eggs in his eyes. And what about the little dog? Did it keep returning to Uncle Gene's dead leg? Would it die before it tried to bite off a chunk? Or would it too expire, right on the dead man's lap?

No, Riley thought. Uncle Gene was not in his trailer. That is, his body might still be, but his soul, or whatever, was elsewhere—or soon would be. It was possible, she thought. Jaybird would've said it wouldn't matter, that what humans feared wasn't death but suffering. No man remembered coming into the world. Neither would any remember his exit.

Before they left the motel, Jaybird had relieved the lobby's continental breakfast of a dozen prepackaged danishes (stowing them giddily in the inside pockets of a green army jacket), and instructed Riley to take a couple extra boxes of Frosted Flakes and an orange. An alert-looking man in glasses and a plaid button-up, sitting beneath a TV where a black CNN anchor discussed the seriousness of identity theft, had eyed them with suspicion. "What?" Jaybird said. "We paid for this shit, did we not?"

Now, Jaybird held a joint between his fingers and steered with a single finger hooked around the steering wheel. The calm manner in which he piloted the truck— the way he casually tapped ash out the cracked window— seemed counterfeit. He glanced every so often into the rear view mirror, as if expecting something there to appear.

"No thanks," Riley said, when he offered her a hit. She felt paranoid enough as it was. She couldn't stop wondering what they'd left behind, what mistakes they'd made. Tire tracks in Gene's driveway. Shoe prints on the kitchen floor. Fingerprints on the rental car agreement. In her mind's eye, she saw an officer lift a strand of hair and place it in a Ziploc bag. The hair would travel to a lab. Scientists would study it under microscopes, determine its DNA. An all-points bulletin would go out. She and Jaybird would be hunted down, shackled, suited, and jailed. Their pictures would appear in that obnoxious newspaper they sold for a dollar at gas stations, the one that featured mug shots of local criminals. Everybody they knew, including her own mother, would think they were trash. And that they would deserve whatever they had coming.

"What's on your mind," Jaybird said.

"Nothing."

"Don't lie."

"I'm just thinking."

"About what?"

"Oh, I don't know. The police. Jail. What I might eat before my lethal injection."

With a fist, Jaybird pushed his chin one way then the other, effectively cracking his neck. "We've been over this," he said. He flicked the roach out the window. "There's only one person that warrants an investigation."

Aunt Wanda, Riley thought. Who knew what recent conflicts, thanks to Gene's lottery winnings, had transpired between them? Maybe the money had lured her, if only for a night, back to his side? It was easy to imagine. Aunt Wanda was unstable and usually broke. She hadn't worked in years, and Riley's mother was convinced that she, Wanda, had a prescription drug problem. She'd also fallen love with a retarded boy. Riley felt bad for her. But, if Riley thought hard enough, she could understand how somebody could fall in love with the boy. He wasn't the worst thing in the world to look at. And it wasn't like he was *retarded* retarded. For instance, he could drive. He had a job at the Home Depot in Blairsville, in receiving. He was sweet. Probably had an insane sex drive. She'd heard that about mongoloids. That wasn't what he was, but still.

If Wanda got convicted for killing Gene, she'd surely be sentenced to life in prison, if not death row. Riley could picture it: for the rest of her days, she'd eat fish sticks and creamed corn from segmented cafeteria trays, trade sexual favors for cigarettes, shots of booze. She might get shanked. She'd want to blame someone, but she wouldn't know who, wouldn't have any idea that it all came down to one thing: if Riley'd kept her big trap shut, none of this would've happened.

Highway 441—the road winding through the Great Smokies—was clotted with traffic. Riley hadn't visited the park since last Halloween, when Jaybird had taken her to the Mysterious Mansion in Gatlinburg, a city whose name he always followed ironically with "Gateway to Paradise." Unlike their previous trip, Jaybird made no remarks about the moss-smothered trunks of trees, didn't discuss how park rangers had injected hemlocks with an antidote to inoculate them from the ravages of the woolly adelgid. He didn't say "chipmunk" whenever a chipmunk scurried across the road. Didn't say that they shouldn't even be allowed to drive through this place, and that the burning of fossil fuels produced tiny airborne particles that dispersed light and erased scenic views. Didn't say that he should be ashamed but wasn't and how sad he guessed that probably was.

Instead, Jaybird cursed the Escalade they'd gotten stuck behind—the one that was failing to reach the park's 45 m.p.h. speed limit and whose ruby taillights brightened whenever it approached anything resembling a curve. That its back window had been plastered with stickers— two stick figure adults and two stick figure kids, an OBX decal, a cartoon of a praying boy, and an Ichthys symbol— only increased his ire. What they needed to make, in his opinion, was a sticker of this exact truck, with all its bull- shit symbols, and then depict one of those Calvin cartoons taking a piss on it. Riley forced a chuckle. Maybe she, too, could pretend everything was normal. She let her arm dan- gle out the open window and practiced not flinching when flying insects pelleted her skin. She waved lazily to a pair of Harley riders who'd parked at a roadside table, saluted when—at the crest of the mountain, at Newfound Gap— the Escalade turned, without signaling, into a parking lot.

"You gotta be kidding me," Jaybird said. Riley thought he was rerouting his indignation, beaming it at the con- vertible that'd swerved in front of them, but then that car sped away, and Jaybird wasn't accelerating. He was frowning at the dash.

"What's wrong?" she said.

"Truck's running hot."

Riley craned her neck. The gauge's arrow pointed directly at the H.

Jaybird coasted into a small lot with a retaining wall. Below them, a creek's dark water was streaked with whitecaps. He popped the hood, went to take a look. White smoke poured out. Riley couldn't see what he was doing.

He climbed back into the truck and slammed the door. "There ain't a goddamn drop of coolant in this mother-fucker," Jaybird said. He ran his hand over his face. He punched the steering wheel. The truck honked pitifully. Smoke cascaded upward. *A signal*, Riley thought. Alerting anybody who cared to know—the police? the Feds? Uncle Gene's ghost?—of their whereabouts.

"What're we gonna do?"

Jaybird shook his head. "Start walking."

"Seriously?"

"It ain't but ten miles."

"Ten?"

"At least."

Riley laughed.

"Don't worry. I wouldn't ask you to come."

"And just what would you expect me to do?"

"Set here. Hard enough for one person to hitch a ride, much less two."

"Mm," Riley said. "Sounds good. Maybe on your way you could get chopped up by a psychopath."

"You got a better plan?"

She didn't.

Jaybird said to lock the doors and sit tight. He didn't slide the gun from the glove box and into his pants. He didn't kiss or hug or fist bump Riley goodbye. He simply hoisted his backpack onto his shoulders, climbed out, and started walking. Or, rather, sauntering: hands gripping his pack-straps, his head swiveled to and fro, as if taking in the view. Riley, who thought she could hear him whistling as he disappeared around a bend in the road, thought about yelling, "Wait!" but reconsidered. She shut her eyes, dug fingernails into her fore-arms. The storm she'd been suppressing rose like hot bouillon inside her. She covered her face with her hands and wept.

Rain fell. Riley counted the splats. At first, it was easy. One. Two. Three four. Five six. Then her count morphed into estimates. For a few dramatic minutes, the world outside was a wash of white light—the sun was out, but it was pouring so hard she couldn't see a foot beyond the windshield. She imagined Jaybird trying to flag down vehicles and none of them stopping, because who wanted to pick up a skinny dude in a sopping T-shirt, through which his nipples were showing? Then—as suddenly as it began—the downpour relented. The asphalt shimmered, as if it'd been formed by the liquefaction and subsequent solidification of pulverized jewels.

To pass the time, Riley ate four hunks of beef jerky from a plastic pouch, nibbling slowly, as if she were in a slow-eating contest. She unwrapped a peppermint and let it dissolve into a wafer before chomping it to smithereens. She unfolded a map of Tennessee, failed to locate her current position. She made a mental list of things she might purchase were she to choose to be utterly selfish and blow a ridiculous amount of money. A brown suede jacket. A piano. An entire collection of vintage, embroidered cowboy shirts. An El Camino. A steak and a baked potato. A blender. A Taser.

In the ashtray, she located Jaybird's roach and lit it. She held hot smoke inside her lungs and inventoried the glove box: a folder in which Jaybird kept the records of the truck's oil changes and tune-ups; a piece of junk mail that'd been printed with the word "Confidential" in a red font that suggested it'd been hand-stamped; a DVD case for a movie called *Final Events,* which, she knew, had been sent to Jaybird by a church his mother had taken him to when he was a kid. According to the movie, Jesus would return to Earth in a city slash spaceship whose skyline resembled a series of golden capital buildings. He would call the wicked to rise up. Then, Satan would assemble an army of the iniquitous, so as to attempt an attack on the Holy City. The wicked would be no match for Jesus, however. His Heavenly fire would consume them.

It didn't sound half bad to Riley, as long as Jesus saved her a place on the spaceship. Assuming she deserved to be rescued. *Blessed are the meek*, she thought. Jesus had said that. Was she meek? She wasn't sure. Poor in spirit? That was more like it.

She took another pull on the roach, inhaled a mouthful of charred weed. Picking bits from her tongue, she wondered if maybe flames from Heaven would be different from Earthly ones: if maybe the Heavenly ones would be kinder, wouldn't hurt as bad.

She opened her phone. It was 12:15. More than two hours had passed. She had no new messages. She sent one to Jaybird: "how much longer?" There was one bar left on her battery icon—a lonely stripe that would soon fade into oblivion. She dug through her backpack for a charger, connected the phone to Jaybird's cigarette lighter. That's when it hit her: Jaybird had taken the keys.

Another hour passed. Every car that rounded the corner symbolized the vehicle that might save Riley from the agony of waiting. But none did. Which meant she had to come to grips with a problem she'd been trying to avoid: for a while now, longer than she'd cared to admit, she'd needed to pee. She opened the driver's side door, pocketed her phone, slid on her backpack, buckled the straps. Inside, she carried a change of clothes, a miniature flashlight, a toothbrush and paste, a clear zippered bag containing mascara and lip gloss, a wallet, the .38 Special with five rounds remaining. And Uncle Gene's lottery winnings.

She crossed the road. There, on the other side, the
woods were dense and steaming. She parted limbs,
stomped briars. Wet leaves licked her arms and face.
Sunlight filtered through branches. The forest canopy
fluttered with golden light, and every few steps she was
showered by still-dripping trees. A hornet—swerving
drunkenly—smacked her forehead, and though it hadn't
stung her she now worried what would happen if one did,
remembering a show on *Animal Planet* where a woman
had suffered dozens of stings, ballooned, suffocated, and
survived long enough to become a vegetable. Standing on
a slope that veered toward a creek, Riley unbuttoned her
jeans, slid them to her ankles, held onto a sapling, and
peed downhill. As she finished, she spotted a Happy Meal
box nestled like a gaudy temple among a bed of ferns. She
opened and immediately dropped it. There was something
black and rotten inside; it took a second for her to realize this furry vegetable patty was somebody's turd. She
half expected someone to laugh. She scanned the woods.
Nobody. She didn't believe in ghosts, but she'd never been
a fan of the woods, which were, she imagined, chock full
of creatures hiding in secret places. She told herself she
would not run, so as not to give anything that might be
watching the impression that she might be afraid. And
then, because she wasn't paying attention, she tripped on
a root, and tumbled toward the stream.

Typical, she thought. She'd opened a hole in her jeans.
Skinned her knee. Gotten dirt in her mouth. Leaves in
her hair. She washed off in the stream, wondered if the
water had been contaminated by boar piss. She guessed
she'd find out.

She had not locked the doors of the truck. At least she
hadn't thought so. But when she tried both door han-
dles—each one multiple times—they wouldn't open.

A black Escalade—similar to the one they'd been following earlier that day—was now parked in the lot. A couple—a man wearing sunglasses, Croakies, and a shirt that said "World's Greatest Dad," and a bleached blonde woman, whose roots were showing and whose shirt declared that she was "Property of Jesus"—were studying a roofed sign when their attention swerved to Riley.

"Everything okay?" the man asked.

"I'm good," Riley said.

"You're bleeding," the man noted, pointing at her knee. And she was. Through the rip in her jeans, a rivulet of dark blood trickled.

The woman snapped her fingers. "Don't move," she said. She opened, then rooted around in the trunk of the Escalade, located a first aid kit, tore open a wipe soaked in disinfectant and dabbed it against Riley's knee. It stung.

"What happened?" the man asked.

"I fell," Riley said. "In the woods."

"You by yourself?" the woman asked.

Riley explained: she and her boyfriend were headed north when their truck overheated. Now he had gone, on foot, to retrieve coolant. The man's brow furrowed. The woman chewed her gum earnestly. Riley worried that they'd think she was making it all up, that they'd assume this wasn't her truck and that she was some sort of vagabond to distrust.

"How long's he been gone?" the woman said.

"A couple hours."

"He have a phone?" the man said.

"He's not answering."

A window in the Escalade descended. An arm hung out the side and knocked impatiently against the door. A voice from inside said, "Cut it out!"

"Want us to give you a ride? It's no problem. We're headed that way."

Riley glanced at the grille of Jaybird's truck. At the headlights. Together, they composed a snout-like face on a head that couldn't care less. As if maybe it'd planned this all along, and was now settling in for some quiet time.

"You have room?" she asked.

"Tons," the man said.

"It's simple," the woman said. She dug through a silver purse excessively bedecked with buckles and straps. "We'll drive you to town. Along the way, we'll keep an eye out for your boyfriend. You'll leave him a note here, so if we cross paths, he'll know where you went."

She handed Riley a pad and a chubby pink pen whose shell housed a universe of glitter suspended in clear fluid.

"Take all the time you need," the man said. He slid a hand onto his wife's back as they walked away.

Riley leaned on the hood of Jaybird's truck, trying to think of what to say. In the air above the paper, she scribbled indecipherable letters. Finally, she forced herself to write: *I went to pee, and your dumb truck locked me out. You have the keys. Didn't feel like standing here looking shady for the next six hours, so I'm hitching a ride to G-burg with some random people. Don't worry. They don't seem totally insane. Will call, assuming they don't sacrifice me and that I'm able to charge my phone. R.*

She lifted a windshield wiper, slid the sloppily folded page beneath it. The blade snapped back on her finger. Impulsively, she punched the glass. Nothing shattered. Her knuckles sang out in pain.

In the Escalade, Riley sat between two kids, a boy and a girl. The girl's shirt said "My Chemical Romance" and featured an image of sullen teenagers with white skin and dyed hair. The girl wore her own hair short and had a silver stud in her nose. Her brother was chubby. His yellow and purple tank top said "Nash" on the back. They introduced themselves. Riley said her name, forgot theirs. The man flicked the turn signal. A tick-tock sounded. Riley imagined a bomb silently exploding. She buckled her seatbelt, and the Escalade lunged onto the road.

"So," Riley said. "Where are ya'll from?"

"Chimneys of Marvin," the boy said.

"Near Charlotte," the mom explained.

The family's house appeared in Riley's mind: It was made of gray brick and had multiple rooflines, all of them steep. Its living room boasted sectional couches, a giant fireplace, and a high-def TV. The man had an office with lots of bookshelves but very few books, maybe a taxidermied wood duck or an assembly of Little League trophies. The master bedroom had a king-size canopy bed, heaped with pillows, many of them bearing tassels.

"And you?" the dad said.

"Happy Top," Riley said.

The dad tilted his head. "Never heard of it."

"Nobody has."

"Sounds like a fun place," the boy said. "Is it really happy?"

"Some days are better than others," Riley replied.

The man laughed. The woman explained that it had been her son's turn to choose the family vacation, and he'd chosen the Smokies. The boy nodded. They'd spent the previous night in Cherokee, where they'd toured the Indian Village and learned about the Trail of Tears.

"So sad," the woman said.

"My dad won money at the casino!" the boy declared.

"For the record," the woman said, "we do not condone gambling or games of chance."

"Guess how much," the boy exclaimed.

"A thousand dollars?" Riley said.

"What? Not that much."

"Okay, a hundred."

"Eighty-two!"

Riley raised her eyebrows. "Nice!"

The announcer on the radio thanked them for listening to CCM, the world's best contemporary Christian station.

"Can you turn this up?" the girl requested.

A singer sang: "I am chosen. I am holy. I am new."

"So," the woman said. "What's your boyfriend's name?"

"Jason," Riley said. The name felt false on her tongue, despite the fact that it was the one he'd been given.

"Hey Mom," the boy said, "did you know that Jason's in the Bible?"

"I sure did."

"He's one of the seventy disciples," said the boy. He fired up a handheld video game, where his avatar used a sniper rifle to blast holes in the heads of kaffiyeh-wearing enemies. Little clouds of digitized mist appeared every time he got one.

Riley watched the green blur of trees outside the window, hugged her backpack tight, and tried not to envision Jaybird's demise. The thought of anything happening to him—if, say, he was walking down this road, which was narrow and basically shoulder-less, and a big truck like this whizzed by, and one of its side-view mirrors clipped him in the head, he might tumble into a ravine, where his body would rot and take weeks to be found, like that girl back home who'd blacked out at the wheel while doing hits of computer dust spray and swerved off an embankment and into a kudzu-choked gully and had basically decomposed by the time anybody discovered her—made her heart ache.

Riley had never told Jaybird that she loved him, even though he said it to her all the time. In fact, he'd said it after their third date. She'd been rinsing a plate of spaghetti in his sink and he'd come from behind to hug her and whispered it in her ear. It'd scared her and he'd seemed to sense that, told her she didn't have to say it back until she felt it like he did. That'd seemed pretty serious to her. Like, there was some sort of pressure to finally feel it, whatever "it" was. And for it to be true. There'd been times when she'd wanted to say it but hadn't, because she feared it might not sound believable, even to herself.

Riley's leg buzzed. She flipped open her phone, frowned at the screen. One new voicemail. How had she not felt the previous call's vibration? She braced herself for the sound of her mother's voice, and thus disappointment.

Hey baby, a voice said. It wasn't her mother. It was Jaybird. *Got your text. Just wanted to call and make sure you're okay. I know it's taking forever.*

There was a pause. She wondered why he was talking like that, as if he were putting on a show. Then she heard laughter in the background and understood. Somebody else was listening.

But you'll never—hey, stop bogarting that thing—you'll never guess (he paused, an inhalation) *who I fucking ran into.*

A storm of static: the phone being handed from one person to another. Then: another voice on the line.

Hey there, Riley! Sorry to make you wait, baby. I kidnapped your boyfriend! Just kidding. I can't believe this jerk left you in the truck. If I were you I would dump—

Riley waited for more, but that was it. Her phone had gone dark. She pressed a series of buttons. It was dead.

There had to be an explanation, but she couldn't think of one. The voice at the other end sounded like Krystal Lovingood. The older woman Jaybird had dated years ago. The one who'd left her husband and kid for a reason she hadn't been afraid to broadcast to anyone who'd listen: they'd bored her to death. The one who'd friended Riley on Facebook. The one Riley'd blocked. She hated having to read her dumb, self-centered posts; they made her picture Krystal and Jaybird together, in her mind, where they were always up to no good. Krystal's photo albums—of which there were many—showcased low-res self-portraits of a glassy-eyed woman in blue eye shadow and lip-gloss, making duck faces or thrusting out a tongue stained with whatever well drink she'd just guzzled, as though she were advertising parts of her body she didn't mind indiscriminately employing. Her captions said things like "Country gone to town!" and "Remove toxic people from your life!" She wore tight shirts that showed off her fake boobs. She'd fried her hair. Her skin had died long ago in a tanning bed. Her fat had been sucked through a straw in an operating room. Either she thought she was hot shit or she was terrified that she might not be. One thing was for sure: she'd proved difficult to satisfy. For instance, according to Jaybird, she'd confessed that she preferred, when making love, to be tied up and choked. Jaybird hadn't liked that much, but he'd gone along with it once or twice, which was part of his problem with Krystal. He'd gone along with a lot of things he should've put a stop to.

In her head now, Riley was giving Jaybird what she, not Krystal, knew he really wanted: to watch two naked women do some weird shit to each other. It was easy to imagine. Riley had her hands around Krystal's throat. Krystal's face was turning blue. Krystal was smiling because, like Jaybird said, she was a gasper who liked to be restrained. If she shut her eyes, Riley could feel Krystal's neck pulse throbbing. She could see herself squeezing harder, even as Krystal's expression changed, her face purpling. The woman's body twisted, trying to get free, but she wasn't going anywhere. Riley was straddling her. She squeezed tighter. Krystal's manicured nails tore at Riley's arms and face, drawing blood. Riley pressed the tip of the gun to Krystal's forehead, could feel it bearing down against the flesh there, against the firmness of the skull. Then: the satisfying kick of the blast.

Good Lord, what was wrong with her? Thinking up junk like this? It made Riley angry to have thought such a thing. But it wasn't her fault. Had Jaybird never left her, she wouldn't be in this position, riding in a car with strangers, carrying a loaded firearm and a butt-load of cash. She had gone from her regular old self to someone who made things happen, not all of them good.

The man pulled into the first restaurant he saw once they reached town: the Burning Bush. Was Riley hungry? Because they'd be glad to buy her a meal. Riley said thanks but she should get going—she needed to locate a charger for her phone. Would she mind if they prayed for her first? She guessed she wouldn't. It might be nice, she thought, to hear a prayer, to believe—if only for a moment—that somebody else knew the magic words that would help her. The man orchestrated a family huddle—one into which Riley was subsumed—and bowed his head. "Dear Lord, please watch over Jason," he began. "Keep him under Your watch and care." As the prayer continued, Riley observed everybody's faces. The boy wrinkled his nose, as if he had an itch. The girl's eyelids fluttered. The woman nodded, whispered, "Yes" whenever she agreed with something that the man was thankful for. Riley felt that the family had retreated momentarily inside a secret communal place—one to which she couldn't gain access. At the end, everybody but Riley said, "Amen," the realization of which caused Riley to worry that maybe she'd canceled the whole thing out.

Gatlinburg's sidewalks were glutted with waddlers. Fat dads. Fat moms. Fat kids, tugging on T-shirts that rode up their bellies. Riley's feet were killing her. Her knee burned where she'd scraped it—maybe, she thought, some kind of flesh-eating bacteria was getting to work. Her body was shellacked in a sweat-sheen. A bank sign claimed it was ninety-six degrees. She was starving, and everywhere she looked, a pancake house appeared. A pancake house with a Conestoga wagon parked on its roof. A pancake house whose awning displayed a cast iron skillet and a stack of flapjacks. A pancake house that resembled a log cabin, a teepee, a dome. But she wasn't about to stop; hunger fueled her indignation, which she would need later. She wasn't naturally flirty or theatrical or wild. But she was pretty sure she could play-act, make all that stuff up, if she wanted. How hard could it be?

She kept going. She stopped at a fake cobblestone path that wound through a series of shops that, collectively, were engaged in a half-hearted impersonation of a Renaissance village, removed her backpack to stow her hoodie inside. It was growing heavier and heavier. Through a massive window, she watched a complicated machine pull taffy—a lurid process that resembled the stretching of greased flesh. She passed disgruntled-looking seniors piloting mobile scooters, a pair of Amish boys with bowl cuts fervently tonguing soft-serve cones. In the distance, an unreliable-looking chairlift lifted people—old and young, fat and thin—to the top of a ridge overlooking the city. Every few blocks, she sought reprieve from the heat inside arcades blinking with red and orange lights, stores selling candied apples, and popcorn dyed blue.

Meanwhile, her phone remained uncharged. It wasn't for the lack of souvenir shops that also sold electronics. Riley had visited half a dozen of these places, eyed mugs bearing Confederate flags and camouflage purses embroidered with buck heads and shirts that spelled "Jesus Christ" using the Coca-Cola font. But she hadn't found

a charger. The kind of phone Riley had, the shop own-
ers explained, was very, very old. Maybe she wanted to
buy a new phone? She'd think about it, she'd said. But the
thought of buying a new one made her feel desperate. And
that was the last thing she wanted to feel.

She located a pay phone. Although she had no coins,
pressing the earpiece to her head helped calm her down.
She reminded herself to be patient. There could be any
number of explanations as to why Jaybird was nowhere
to be found, the number one being: he wasn't here. He
might've passed them in another car on their way down
the mountain. He might never have gotten her note. He
might've run into a police roadblock. Or maybe he'd asked
to drive Krystal's car and she'd gone with him, taken hold
of his crotch, making him swerve, and they'd ended up in
a ditch.

Riley thought about calling her mom. Her mom would
say, "How is everything?" and Riley would say, "Oh,
everything's hunky-dory," which long ago had been a code
they'd agreed to use if, for example, one of them was being
held hostage and told by her kidnappers, when answering
the phone, to play it cool.

"We're in Maine," she said, to the mouthpiece. "It's a
strange place. Everything's backwards. They drive on
the other side of the road. They go inside when the sun
shines. They stay out in the rain. They eat eggs for supper
and roast beef for breakfast. They say goodbye instead
of hello."

"Please deposit fifty-five cents," the phone said.

She hung up the receiver.

She found the World's Greatest Dad and his family standing in front of Ripley's Haunted Adventure. He was waving and calling her name.

"Oh," she said. "Hi again."

"Ever find your boyfriend?" the boy asked.

Riley tried to think of a lie but couldn't. "No," she said.

"Get that phone charged?" the man inquired.

"I'm working on it."

The woman, clearly the family documentarian, wanted everybody to come this way, because she wanted to get a group picture—"You too, Riley!"—beside Stumpy. Stumpy was a legless torso in white makeup and top hat and fingerless gloves who hovered inside a wooden box. His spinal column dangled beyond the tips of his vest like a tail. His job was to shout randomly at people who didn't notice him. According to the boy, he'd made the man scream like a little girl.

Riley couldn't determine how to use the man's smartphone so she told him the number; he punched it in and handed it back. She excused herself, stood next to an illuminated sign advertising a mountain of assorted candies. Jaybird's phone rang once then went straight to voicemail, which meant one of several things: a. he was calling her; b. he was calling someone else; or c. *his* phone had died. "Jaybird, it's me," Riley said, after the beep. "Call me on this number. My phone's dead."

"Guess you're stuck with us for a while," the man said. This observation seemed to please him. He fanned himself with a brochure promoting gospel singers in sequined suits and unitards.

"I appreciate it," Riley said. She was forming an alliance with these innocent people. They had no idea who she really was. That she was carrying more money in her backpack right now than she'd spent in her entire life. That she'd left a dead man and an orphaned dog in her wake. She didn't want to threaten them with the .38. But who knew what would happen next? If one of them tried to mess with her somehow, she might not have a choice.

·

At the family's hotel—a string of two-story, orange-roofed buildings, whose balconies faced a roaring creek—the woman wouldn't let anyone walk barefoot on the carpet. From her unzipped suitcase, she provided flip-flops. "You don't know whose feet have been there."

"Feet are the tip of the iceberg," the man said.

"Mom," the girl said, "they have maids."

"Yeah, but there's no way of knowing what kinds of corners they cut."

Riley requested the use of the bathroom. Her body felt like it was teeming with microorganisms. At the sink, she unwrapped a slender rectangle of soap, washed her arms and face. An hour before, they'd been strapped into in a 4D Motion Ride designed to convince them that they were trapped in a runaway mining car. At one point, the car launched itself off the rails, through a wall, and onto the side of a mountain. Actual fake snow snowed down on them. The lights came up. A place on Riley's leg, where the fake snow had landed, looked like it'd been jizzed on. Soon, it turned into a kind of crystallized powder. Now, she scrubbed vigorously.

When she reappeared, the boy wanted to show Riley the pool. The man said she probably didn't want to see the pool, but Riley said it was okay. The woman told everybody to go ahead, she'd catch up. She wanted to unpack a few things first.

"Don't you wanna leave that backpack here?" she asked Riley. "That thing looks heavy."

"Um," Riley said, "okay." She didn't want to be weird about it, so she slid it off. Set it against the wall. Stretched.

"See?" the woman said.

Riley rubbed her shoulders. It was true. Setting out with the boy and girl and their father, she felt light on her feet.

The pool was inside a tall outbuilding. A little bridge arched over the water. A Jacuzzi worked itself into a lather. A foamy stream, presumably pumped from the pool, cascaded over a fake rock wall. "This is the coolest!" the boy said. "Hey guys, watch me do a cannonball!" The girl took off her boots and a pair of socks upon which skulls and crossbones had been knitted, and stuck her feet in. The man sat at a glass table, tapping his phone screen. The air was unbearably humid, the windows opaque with steam.

"Bet you didn't think you'd be spending your Wednesday night like this," the dad said.

"Nope," Riley said.

"Who wants a snack?" he bellowed.

Riley said she was good. The girl failed to respond. The boy yelled "Doritos!" The man hoisted himself out of his chair.

The mom, Riley knew, would look. There was no doubt about it. If Riley were a mom, *she'd* look. She'd poke her head out the door and see if the coast was clear, then chain the door. She'd dig feverishly into the backpack. Within seconds, she'd find the money and the gun. She might not put two and two together, but she'd know something was up. Or off. Definitely wrong. The woman claimed to be— and thus in all likelihood was—the property of Jesus. But she wouldn't call the police. Surely not. After all, it wasn't a crime to carry a gun. Wasn't a crime—Riley didn't think—to travel with large sums of cash. But the woman would have to do something. At least write down the name and address that appeared on Riley's driver's license that she'd find in her wallet, which was sitting in the top pouch of the backpack. She wouldn't know what to do with it now, but she'd hold onto it. At some point, she'd enter the information into a search engine. Not much would come up. A listing for some high school basketball statistics. A listing on a "people search" site. But she wouldn't be able to let it go. She'd have a feeling. And, being the property of Jesus, she'd feel compelled to do something. She'd keep checking. At some point, she'd go back to the basketball page, maybe because it had the most information. She'd click "Home" on that page. Headlines would appear. Riley's hometown paper. Something about a man getting shot. A robbery. Then she'd know.

The World's Greatest Dad returned with snacks. From somewhere on his person, the notes of a Steve Miller song began to play. He unclipped his phone from his belt.

"Hello?" he said. "Sure. Hold on just a second." He raised the phone toward Riley. "It's for you," he said, smiling.

Riley took the phone outside. She stood in a bed of mulch. Across the street, at another outdoor pool, a big woman holding a pigtailed toddler waded in the shallow end, tapped the ash of her cigarette into a beer can.

"Hello?" Riley said.

"Thank you, Lord," Jaybird said.

"Excuse me?"

"You're alive."

"Yeah," Riley replied.

"I didn't know what had happened to you."

"Tell me about it."

"You still in Gatlinburg?"

"Standing outside a hotel pool. You?"

"In front of some place called . . . World of Illusions."

"Where's Krystal?"

"Oh my God," Jaybird said. His voice sounded shaky. "That girl is insane."

"What happened?"

Jaybird inhaled deeply. "Okay, so she stopped when she saw me, right? I tell her what the problem is and she

says she'll give me a ride. Only she don't want to go to
Gatlinburg. She's headed to Cherokee. Fine, I say. Either
way, I've got to buy some coolant. So she starts driving
like a bat out of hell. I mean, we must've hit eighty-five on
some of the stretches. I swear, she was passing on double
yellows. Laughing the whole time."

"Huh."

"I'm telling you. She's insane."

"That's what you like, right?"

"What are you talking about?"

"I'm talking about you. And Krystal."

Silence.

"Don't tell me you're insinuating that we—"

"That you what."

"Jesus, Riley. She's got a boyfriend."

"And what about you?"

"What about me?"

"What have you got?"

"Do you need to be told?"

"Maybe I do."

"Listen. Can we just pick somewhere to meet?"

Riley didn't answer. She wanted him to think she was
thinking about it.

"Hello?"

"You left me," she said.

"I know, I know. And I'm sorry, baby. I really am. It was
stupid. We should've stayed together. I wasn't thinking."

"Stay where you are," Riley said. "I'll find you."

The door to the hotel room was cracked. Riley knocked
and, as she waited, studied the business card the man
had given her. "Global Solutions," the card said. It was
embossed with a toll-free number and a picture of a globe
with a face. The globe was wearing a mortarboard hat
and solving a quadratic equation.

A voice said, "Come in." Riley entered. The woman had drawn back the comforter on one of the beds and was sitting Indian-style upon the sheets. She'd tied her hair in a ponytail. Her pajama pants were imprinted with flowers. On the TV, a group of prisoners were tarring a roof. A miniature bottle of Zinfandel stood next to a fluted glass.

"Hey," Riley said. "It's me. I'm just back to get my stuff."

"Oh?"

"Yeah," Riley said.

The backpack sat where she'd left it. It appeared to be untouched. Riley bent down and unzipped it. Glanced at the woman's face, searching for any expression that might betray her. But the woman, taking a sip of her wine, stared calmly at the television. Riley dug through layers of clothes, located the bag of money, the stacks of bills, the gun. There was no way to know whether the woman had rummaged through the backpack, and only one way to be sure that, if she had, she wouldn't say anything to anyone about what she found there. Riley squeezed the gun's handle, as if testing out the idea. But then Uncle Gene's blood-streaked face appeared in her mind. The open, hanging mouth. The eyes glazed and dead. She released her grip. Quickly drew back her hand.

As she stood to shoulder her backpack, the woman asked, "Did you hear from your boyfriend?" Eyebrows raised, she looked genuinely hopeful.

"Yeah," Riley said. "He ended up calling. On your husband's phone."

"And he's okay?"

"He's fine. He said he, like, passed out or something. He bent down to tie his shoe and when he stood up," she snapped her fingers, "and it was lights out."

The woman frowned. "That doesn't sound fine to me."

Riley shrugged. "It happens sometimes. When his sugar gets low."

"Excuse me?"

"Low blood sugar. He doesn't eat like he should. Anyway, I should get out of your hair."

"Wait," the woman said. She swung her legs over the edge of the bed, slid her feet into flip-flops, and shuffled across the room.

Before Riley could protest, the woman gave her a hug. She squeezed her long and hard. "It was so nice to meet you," the woman said. The woman's neck smelled minty. Her body was soft and warm, like velvety bread.

"You, too," she said.

"Hey," the woman said. "Before you leave, would it be okay if we prayed together?"

The woman held out her hands. It took a moment for Riley to understand that she was supposed to take hold of them. They were warm. The woman shut her eyes. "Dear Lord," she said, "We thank You today for the chance to meet this wonderful girl. We know that You are Author of all, and we ask that You keep her in Your loving hands—"

Riley stared unabashedly at the woman. There were only a few people she had scrutinized from this close up, and she did so now only because she knew that as long as the woman was praying, she wasn't going to open her eyes. The purity of her obliviousness invited further investigation. So Riley studied the woman's face—the shut eyelids, the flexing hollows of her nostrils, the place next to her temple that looked like a bird had left its claw-print in the supple mud of her skin. If Riley looked closely enough, maybe she too could learn how to unselfconsciously retreat inside herself, to a private sanctuary where she too could find assurance and grace. The woman's face, however, refused to divulge its secrets. Maybe, Riley thought, it didn't have any. Maybe that's where its tranquility originated. It was a face with nothing to hide.

"In Jesus's name," the woman said, "Amen."

•

The sidewalks were packed with bloated fools and shriek-
ing kids. People eating caramel apples. People with soul
patches and ponytails. These were people who had just
played eighteen holes of Hillbilly Golf or swum in a hotel
pool or disembarked from a jam-packed shuttle bus.
People whose phones stored blurry pictures of the jellyfish and eels and hammerhead sharks they'd visited at
the aquarium. People Riley would never see again, who
knew nothing about her. To them, she was a woman with
a backpack, a hiker maybe, somebody in need of a shower,
but certainly nobody to fear. A regular person, like she
once had been. Her shoulders ached. She rubbed her neck,
rolled strings of dirt from her skin, flicked them away. She
wanted to wriggle free of the backpack for good, peel off
her sticky clothes, scrub herself clean in a cloud of steam.

Then, in the distance: a siren.

The police, she thought.

Had the woman called them?

The siren—a wail of stupidity—faded.

She picked up her pace.

She found Jaybird where he said he'd be, in front of a
building that had been constructed to look as if a small
plane had crashed into its side. Riley felt dialed in. Fired
up. Like she might walk the hot knife of herself through
the meat of another human body and leave two sizzling
halves behind.

A sign read WORLD OF ILLUSIONS. In the museum's
doorway, Jaybird was flanked by two old women. One had
a map. The other was tonguing lavender ice cream from
a waffle cone. Jaybird pointed to the map, elbowed the
woman like they were old pals. The woman laughed, patted Jaybird's shoulder, and led her friend away.

"What a nice boy," Riley said.

"Hey," he said, as she approached. "Listen, baby, I'm really—"

She grabbed one of his hands and tugged. "Com'ere," she said.

"What is it?"

"I have something to show you."

"So show me."

"Not here," she said. She scanned the parking lot next to the museum. "Over there." She headed for the shadow cast by a large dumpster. Led him to an alley behind a T-shirt emporium. Pavement glittered in the dim light of a street lamp.

"Why all the secrecy?" Jaybird said. His face glistened. His cheeks were shiny, as if he'd rubbed them with pork fat.

Riley glanced over her shoulder. Nobody. She slid off her pack, opened it. Shoved her hand inside, drew out the plastic bag. Handed it to Jaybird.

He frowned. "What's this?"

"Open it," she said.

He peered inside. He blinked. "No way," he said.

Riley rummaged through her backpack.

"Is there more?"

"Yes and no."

Jaybird hooted.

"Shhh!" she said.

"Sorry," he whispered. He looked gleeful, like he had a couple of weeks before, when, on a night she'd taken a gravity bong hit and stationed herself in front of *Storage Wars*, he'd yelled at her to come look. She'd found him standing on his back porch, holding a possum by its tail. A garbage can had toppled. Trash was everywhere. The greasy mammal squirmed and hissed in the light. The porch had become a kind of stage, upon which Jaybird was performing, the animal a creature that served at his leisure, until he swung it into the yard, and it wobbled away.

"Holy shit," he said now, shaking his head. "Why in the world didn't you—"

She withdrew the gun from the backpack and, in a fluid motion, cocked it. Her hands didn't even shake as she pointed it at him.

"What the fuck?" Jaybird said. He squinted, as if she were shining a blindingly bright light at his face. "Don't point that thing at—"

"It's all yours," she said.

"All what?"

"The money," she said. "You earned it."

"This is crazy," Jaybird said.

She extended her arm. The gun was close enough for him to knock it from her hand. She sort of hoped that he would. If he whacked it away, she thought, maybe that'd be some kind of sign—one indicating that her plan wasn't as good as she'd thought. She could claim the whole thing was some kind of test that he'd aced, and they could go back to who they'd been before all this happened. In half an hour, they could be high and romping on a hotel bed, their bodies sticky with the champagne they'd showered themselves in. But Jaybird didn't move. Riley could see now that he wouldn't. He had the guts to shoot a man in the heart for next to nothing but he couldn't reach out and disarm the woman he claimed to love. She clenched her jaw and backed up.

"Riley," Jaybird whispered. "Baby."

"Don't," she said.

"Wait," Jaybird said. "Where are you going?"

"Home."

"What about Maine?"

"What about it?"

"You and me, remember? Vacationland. And now all this." He held up the money.

She shook her head. *Maine*, she thought. She couldn't believe she'd been stupid enough to think they'd ever end up there.

"You have to promise me something," Riley said.

"Anything."

"Promise you'll never come home."

"Hey now. I can't just—"

"I mean it. If I see you again . . . it won't be like this."

Jaybird tilted his head. "What'll it be like?"

"Ugly."

She would've bet every last bill that Jaybird would follow her, that he'd yell "Wait!" and "Come on!" and "This is stupid." She even gave him the chance. She didn't run away; she walked. *One word*, she thought. If he said her name just once she would turn around. But he didn't make a peep. Hadn't guessed that the gun's chambers were empty. That she'd tapped out the remaining bullets into the trash can inside the bathroom of the Donut Friar. That she wouldn't have shot him then or ever. He'd bought her performance. Which was maybe a good thing. If Jaybird believed that she was brave enough to leave him, maybe she wasn't just acting. Maybe she was just playing herself.

Forward she went. It wasn't hard. As long as she could keep her eyes dry and put one foot in front of the other, she could blend in, look like she'd come to this town for fun and games. She waved to a toddler, seemingly parentless, who stood outside Adventure Golf, pointing at a mannequin dressed like a quintessential explorer. At Aunt Mahalia's Candies, she used a wadded up five-dollar bill—the only cash she had—and bought a piece of fudge from a boy wearing mascara. She didn't know which one she wanted, so she asked the boy, who said he preferred the regular plain kind. She took a bite. Her mouth was flooded with sweetness. Her eyes watered. *Too much*, she thought, and tossed the remainder into the street.

She went as far as she could—past the shooting gallery; past the giant marble ball spinning in front of Ripley's Believe It or Not Museum, where delighted children shrieked as they petted it; past Fabulous Chalet Inn; past Gateway Market—until she came to the last intersection, the last traffic light. The little town didn't go on forever, and neither did its lights. A national park—an entire wilderness—stood between where she was now and where she wanted to go. Of course, getting there was only part of it. She'd have to explain things to her mother, spin some lies about Jaybird that the woman would find hard to believe, if only because he'd seemed like such a sweet and kind-hearted boy. She'd have to suffer all the indignities of getting her job back, occupying her old room, spending the evenings in the company of a show whose game board was a slow reveal of worthless phrases. And on top of it all, she'd have to carry the secret of what had happened wherever she went. That wouldn't be easy. What choice did she have but to bury the secret deep, plant it like a bone in the dark? Someday, maybe enough time would pass so that she could dig it back up. And there it'd be: a terrible story she could tell without fear, because, by then, it would have all happened to somebody else.

ACKNOWLEDGMENTS

Thanks to friends who gave many of these stories their
first reads: Nic Brown, Fred D'Aguiar, Ed Falco, Kevin
Moffett, Chris Offutt, Scott Sanders, and Joe Scallorns.
Thanks to editors at the literary magazines where many
of these stories first appeared: Gabriel Blackwell at *The
Collagist*, Robert S. Fogarty at *Antioch Review*, Michael
Koch at *Epoch*, Sam Ligon at *Willow Springs*, Matt
Williamson at *Unstuck*. Thanks to Nat Jacks at Inkwell.
Thanks to Karen Braziller and Lexi Freiman for such
ridiculously smart, thorough editing. And thanks always
to my family, to Kelly and Elijah.

A NOTE ABOUT THE AUTHOR

MATTHEW VOLLMER is the author of *Future Missionaries of America*, a collection of stories, as well as *inscriptions for headstones*, a collection of essays. He is the editor of *A Book of Uncommon Prayer*, an anthology of invented invocations; and co-editor (with David Shields) of *Fakes: An Anthology of Pseudo-Interviews, Faux-Lectures, Quasi-Letters, "Found" Texts, and Other Fraudulent Artifacts*. His work has appeared widely, in *The Paris Review, Ploughshares, Glimmer Train, Tin House, Virginia Quarterly Review, Epoch, The Best American Essays, The Pushcart Prize* anthology, and elsewhere. Vollmer directs the undergraduate creative writing program at Virginia Tech.

PHOTOGRAPH BY TODD WEMMER